Wilfred Woollam

Child Illa

And other Poems

Wilfred Woollam

Child Illa
And other Poems

ISBN/EAN: 9783337158088

Printed in Europe, USA, Canada, Australia, Japan

Cover: Foto ©Andreas Hilbeck / pixelio.de

More available books at **www.hansebooks.com**

CHILD ILLA

and Other Poems

BY

WILFRED WOOLLAM, M.A., LL.M.

(Late of St. Peter's College, Cambridge)

AUTHOR OF "WITH THE HELP OF THE ANGELS," "THE FRIENDS OF
INNISHEEN," "ALL FOR NAUGHT," ETC.

SHEFFIELD

J. ARTHUR BAIN

LONDON

SIMPKIN, MARSHALL, HAMILTON, KENT & CO., LTD.

1898

CONTENTS

PREFACE

For permission to reprint many of the smaller and earlier poems in this volume, the writer begs to thank the editors of *The Cornhill*, *Temple Bar*, *The Graphic*, *The Guardian*, *The Wesleyan Methodist Magazine*, *Cassell's Magazine*, *The Quiver*, *The Girl's Own Paper*, and *The Monthly Packet*.

The longer poems, and most of those hitherto unpublished, were written during the last eight years. The earnest wish of the writer is that that portion of the press which considered his fiction worthy of serious attention may not ignore the labours to which he has given greater and more constant love for a longer time. He even ventures to hope that in readers of poetry he may find the public to which those reviewers—not a few among the most influential—so kindly commended his novels without any marked success.

Dedication

———◦⊹◦———

TO ELEANOR, MY SISTER

THINGS left of freights my life's sent out,
   Of freights sent out to me,
Some fondly stored, and some, I doubt,
   Sad salvage of the sea—-
Things left of all I've cared about,
   I give them all to thee.

Take it, in whose kind heart and vast
   Still rocks the peace of mine,
This *débris* of my golden Past,
   The bits that still may shine:
Swept up, where else should all be cast—
   Into whose lap but thine?

Gladness that made it toys of song;
   And grief ground into verse;
Mad things thine image kept from wrong,
   And bad from being worse;
Good—what there are—grown-up and strong,
   Because thou wast their nurse.—

Take them, these fragments of my years,
   Who gave whole years to me—
Worthy, perchance, some smiles and tears;
   Would that some bits might be
Worthy the touch that Time reveres;
   Would one were worthy thee.

Child Illa

I.

'Twas in an ancient land, I wot,
　　When it boots none to know :—
Over the turf and by the surf,
　　In sun and rain and snow,
Careless and calm in his scorn of harm,
　　A knight rode to and fro.

For seven years had he ridden alone,
　　Nor squire nor groom had he ;
But letters from the king he bore
　　And the mien of high degree ;
He never, I trow, lacked seemly foe
　　And hospitality.

And never twice o'er festive board
    His smile or jest was thrown ;
Who knew him by sight, would say, when the
      knight
    Had supped and saddled and flown,
" The knight that hides his name, and rides
    His tameless steed alone ! "

Tho' maids had called him beautiful,
    Men said his strength was vast,
On Valour's prize and Beauty's eyes
    But one quick glance he cast :—
" Not there ! " he sighed ; and his steed's hoofs
      cried,
    " The past ! the past ! the past ! "

So bold and free as on rode he,
    A sad song fain to sing,
Musing upon his heritage,
    Promised him of the king,
He came to a castle by the sea,
    When the bloom was on the ling.

" No more ! no more ! no more ! " sighed he,
   And looked at the castle gay,
" What were my heritage to me?
   What if it came to-day?
O Christ, my King, for the heritage
   That fadeth not away ! "

II.

For seven days who for seven years
   Had but drawn rein to rest,
The knight had stayed, in that castle made
   A glad and welcome guest :—
With thought dream-wrought and passion-swayed
   Child Illa filled his breast—

Rivers of thought reflecting stars,
   Placid and pure and vast :
A dream, a song of love kept strong
   And radiant to the last :—
The dream of old that came, the song
   That came to him—and passed.

Child Illa on her own domain,
   Of all with rev'rence styled !—

Mistress, both of their hearts and wills,
　　Tall, fair, and heav'nly mild :—
" The ripe red rose of womanhood ;
　　White-hearted as a child ! "

So mused the knight, thrilled by the light
　　Of those pure eyes a-shine—
Wondrous beneath her wild gold hair,
　　Above her smile divine :—
" Now king, for me my heritage,
　　She shall be mine—be mine ! "

III.

The knight sat by Child Illa's side,
　　And thought the wide world sweet.
All he had been, in word, act, mien,
　　That maiden had found meet.
" God wot," he sighed, " I'm mystified
　　With rapture so complete."

He told her strange, wild tales of war ;
　　To him her harp she played ;
The heather-hills they two had roamed,
　　The sea-shore and the glade ;

And in the silent chapel dim
   She by his side had prayed.

And soon a rumour reached their ears
   Of strange knights in the glade—
Of battle there ; and at her fears
   He smiled and touched his blade.
" God speed that fight," said the joyous knight ;
   " And shield thee," sighed the maid.

So nigh, and ever yet more nigh,
   Their hearts together came,
Till by a pine-roofed lonely shrine
   The knight told her his name :
" None know it," said the knight—said she,
   " It will be known to fame."

" 'Tis seven years gone since one," said he,
   " Has called me Dondelume."
" But thus would I thee call," said she,
   " ' Scatterer of the gloom ! ' "
The knight he thought that pine the tree
   Of Paradise in bloom.

" Seven years ago, against the foe.
   I rode at the king's side,
When he promised me my heritage,
   That I might take a bride ;
But I took the part, with a broken heart,
   A nameless knight to ride."

" The king my name had honoured still ;
   But, in my grief and gloom,
I vowed that none who knew me not
   Should call me Dondelume."
" I know thee ; sad and strange thy lot,
   ' Scatterer of the gloom ! ' "

IV.

Now heralds cried afar the news
   Of battle by the glade.
And wild that proud knight's bosom swelled
   Whene'er the bugles brayed—
With laurels to ride for his beauteous bride,
   Or in his grave be laid !

With burning love he looked on her ;
   She looked at him and smiled ;

She never dropped her wondrous eyes,
   Her face unearthly mild.
"God !" moaned the knight, "she understands ;
   Or is she all a child ? "

He knew she loved him—loved his voice,
   Loved to be at his side,
Loved to caress his fiery steed,
   · None else could bit or ride ;
"But Heav'ns," moaned he, " Does the child
     see
'Tis she or Death my bride ? "

" For seven years have I tarried not ;
   Two weeks I tarry here ! "
Said she, " Those weeks to me have been
   The best for many a year."
" Soon, soon, comes bliss or death to me— "
   " Bliss," and she dropped a tear.

V.

The pallid moonlight threw its beams
   On weapons in the glen,

From whence swelled high the clank and cry
    Of battle-loving men ;
But one lone knight had dreams of a fight
    He never could dream again.

Away upon the wild sea-shore
    The nameless knight strode he,
Shouting " Child Illa " to the roar
    And foam-flash of the sea—
" ' Child Illa,' and the light of yore
    For me, for me, for me ! "

VI.

The last pale stars were taking flight ;
    The day had streaked the sky ;
From the castle wall the nameless knight
    Watched troops of knights go by—
Child Illa had said, when the night was
    dead,
    Thither to him she'd hie.

Long had his charger pawed the ground ;
    His arms and his armour grand,

A picture of might, he stood bedight,
   Flowers in his ungloved hand ;
But his love delayed, and the bugles brayed—
   He could not understand !

"Quick," to a maid of the castle he cried,
    "To Lady Illa, and say :—
"White thoughts and bloom from Sir Donde-
      lume,
   Whose knighthood forbids him stay ;
And for Jesu's sake, good speed now make,
   To tell me she's well this day."

One minute, and straight came a page.
   (Child Illa's friends stood nigh)—
" My lady's thanks to the stranger knight,
   Her compliments and good-bye ;
Be Christ his stay throughout this day,
   And shield him till he die."

Then slowly, with fair speech and grace,
   He mounted and turned away,
A courteous knight to all in sight,
   Courteous all were they ;

A last light word, and away he spurred,
His face and his heart as clay.

VII.

"The stranger knight ! The stranger knight !
Her compliments and good-bye,"
Arrow-like voices shot him through
From shadows sweeping nigh,
As never horse in headlong course
Bore rider who rode to die.

Out of the mist then came a form ;
Out of the roar a cry :—
"Not Dondelume ! Not Dondelume !
Not him for whom I sigh."
The ghost it had Child Illa's voice,
Child Illa's soft blue eye.

"Who then ? "—The mad knight checked his
horse—
"What hast thou dreamt—been told ? "
The ghost had fled ; a strange voice said,
Withering, mocking, cold :—
"A wavering, mild, hand-guided child,
Freak-cast in woman's mould ! "

"Lies," cried the knight, "her mien proves
     might!"—
   "Her worth is great in gold!"—
"Aye, fiend, and gems, whose radiance
   And wealth can not be told:
The riches incorruptible!"
     The voice said "To be sold!"

"Fool!"—But the knight laughed bitterly:
   The asp had stung his brain.
A blast of bugles rent the air,
   But his charger pranced in vain:—
"Christ, slept my heart seven years from joy,
   To wake in raging pain?"

"What *is* she? What am I? and what
   The meaning of my doom?
Oft in thy sight a shameful knight
   Thro' peril and in gloom;
But what, that man or ghost should mock
   The name of Dondelume?"

Then came a voice—Child Illa's face
   Seen fair as in the past—

" Peace, Dondelume—light in the gloom !
 What if the gloom still last ?
Ride on nor rail ; Earth's loves brief, frail ;
 Heav'n's loves rest safe and vast ! "

VIII.

The tide of fight was reddening fast,
 And rolling fierce and free,
When Montdevaleur's death-filmed eye
 Yet once more turned to see
Who—a tow'r of pride—where the bravest
  died—
 The calm, bold knight might be.

And Dondelume saw that white scarred face,
 To fear and to favour proof—
" God grant, great knight, thy *coup de grace*
 Come not from a horse's hoof."
And seizing his rein, he battled amain,
 Till they rode on the sward aloof.

Than Montdevaleur bolder knight,
 And truer none shall see ;

His emblem was a blood-red hand,
　His motto *cœur-de-lis.*
O'er saddle-bow, never I trow,
　Bowed godlier knight than he.

"Wouldst try his sword, Sir Dondelume,
　Men called the blood-red hand?
Its gleam they knew, but the charm that slew
　They did not understand :—
Behold it shine !　Sir Knight 'tis thine
　If thou can'st wield the brand.'

" Breathe on it," said the dying knight,
　"And kneel thee on the sward.
I' faith no blot : thou hast dimmed it not !
　Commend me to my Lord ;
Quick, and then fly—that once more I
　May see men flee my sword."

"Yet a moment stand: It will pierce his hand
　Who e'er forgets his part.
And now in truth (God bury my youth !)
　I feel of its stabs the smart."

And Dondelume read what the gemmed hilt
    said,
  "Blessèd the pure in heart."

IX.

Long through the seething lanes of death,
    Round thickets of the dead,
Sir Dondelume his wild horse wheeled ;
    Oft o'er his hand blood-red,
A magic spark, men paused to mark
    The flash that his sabre shed.

But twice amazed, his arm upraised,
    He'd swerved as if in fear,
Not from the brand in a foeman's hand,
    An arrow hiss in his ear—
"A battle of knights where no bowman fights,"
    Said Dondelume, "Treachery clear !"

And now to breathe his reeking horse,
    He leaned upon his blade,
When a black-mailed knight with plume snow-
      white,
    His hand upon it laid.

Unheard his tread, and the horse he led
  Nor champed, nor hoof-dint made.

"Sir Dondelume!" The knight's cheek paled,
  But his hand had gripped his sword,
And he measured the foe from his plume of
    snow
  Down to the bloody sward—
"When we've won or lost"—and his breast
    he crossed—
  "In the name of our good Lord!"—

"When we've lost or won by the setting sun!"
  And the dark knight bowed his head—
"Fair knight, what fear to find me near,
  Who oft came near—and fled?
An I bide to-day—fear'st thou false play?
  For us both 'tis as God hath said."

And Dondelume eyed his sombre foe,
  "Now courteous knight and just!"
Then a shaft came deft, which his brain had
    cleft;
  But the dark knight's hand outthrust,

More quick than thought that arrow caught,
　　And crumbled to fiery dust.

"*That* shaft was not for thee; or sure
　　It had not struck my hand!
A noble steed is thine, Sir Knight—
　　As swift as song and grand;
And the blade this day that hews his way,
　　The best blade in the land!"

"Thinkest thou, good Sir Dondelume,
　　We e'er have *foemen* been?
Thee oft I've met; but ne'er seen yet
　　Stretched silent on the green—
That time I bide, with thee to ride—
　　Ride with thee off the scene!"

"Not mine that arrow, no, nor mine
　　The bow from whence it came;
Had'st thou then died, thus had I come;
　　Betimes I come with shame.
To men here meeting the same end
　　That end comes not the same."

Sir Dondelume bowed silently;
　The dark knight calmly smiled,
" To thee, fair knight, fair knight come I,
　To children as a child.
The image that men make me, why,
　Why have men *me* reviled?"

" And now, Sir Knight, God speed, and fight
　Till—I know not, not I—
But this to-day was I bade say,
　To hearten thee when nigh,
' Bliss fills thy breast, or thou hast rest
　Ere stars have strewn that sky!'"

"'Thou know'st the shrine by the lonely
　　　pine——"
　" Know it," the mad knight cried—
"'There, if not stretched upon this field,
　After the battle ride:
So shalt thou meet Child Illa sweet,
　And she shall be thy bride."

X.

The battle's hottest blinding blaze
　Had licked the blood-soaked field.

3

From swathes of silent trampled breasts
   Flashed fallen spear and shield.
In the last wild wave—one deep red grave—
   The king's foes sank and reeled.

And on the crest of that wave's breast,
   Known to his king, and known
Through all that fight as the rallying light,
   Where his wild horse had flown :
Dondelume there—his fame carved fair ;
   His heritage for his own !

XI.

The sun's last ray showed, ghastly—gay
   Stained banners, broken arms,
Glad gallant knights, sad sickening sights :
   War's horrors and its charms—
Proud breasts hope-thrilled; and gored breasts
      stilled
   To all hopes and alarms.

Then many a knight's fair name rang out
   For the king to know his doom ;

But none, I ween, like his who'd been
  Light in that battle gloom—
Afar and nigh, till it seemed the sky
  Had cried "Sir Dondelume!"

But sight nor sound of him they found;
  The king but came to know,
When the fight was won, by the setting sun,
  Dondelume's face aglow,
With sign nor say he had spurred away,
  As he'd spurred him on the foe.

XII.

Beside the bracken-bordered road
  Where moorland met the wood,
The great green pine, and flower wreathed
    shrine
  Lifelong companions stood.
In the pine's gloom lay Dondelume,
  Stand he no longer could.

On the brown bracken leaves he lay,
  Washed of war's blood and mire

His armour and his arms lay nigh—
  Things of fulfilled desire :
Child Illa had not come to him,
  He asked but to expire.

But hark ! a rustling near the shrine ;
  The step as of a child !
Her wondrous eyes more wonderful,
  Her mild sweet face more mild,
Child Illa came and looked on him,
  She looked on him—and smiled.

"Dondelume !" To his side she crept ;
  His heart leapt at her tread.
Then sweetly she on bended knee,
  Low bent her golden head—
She kissed, childwise, his mouth and eyes ;
  He smiled—and he was dead.

Dead ? Did she dream it ? Could she see
  The blood-stain on his vest ?
Yea, and quick drew, tho' tenderly,
  An arrow from his breast—
"Child Illa" on that shaft read she,
  And sighed—a sigh of rest.

Child Illa, she, for those few weeks,
  (How, none will ever know)
And hers the shaft that slew him; hers
  The little golden bow—
She drew it from beneath her robes,
  Her robes now as of snow.

Shining, above her shining hair,
  She held it in her hand;
And round her straight was clustered there
  A white-robed virgin band—-
To mourn the doom of Dondelume,
  The dead knight calm and grand?

Nay, all their eyes and breasts aglow
  With wonder and delight,
Flutt'ring with fearless awe they watched
  Two cavaliers bedight,
From the moorland glow to the glade below
  Pass still as day to night—

A sombre knight with snow-white plume;
  And a knight newly made,
Firm in his seat and straight, by whom
  A gleam danced down the glade—

Death's shadow ; and Sir Dondelume
With Montdevaleur's blade !

Death's shadow ?   Where then, what was
   Death ?
That white-robed filmy throng
Broke, scattered bloom-like by a breath,
   Save bloom here hath no song ;
And the voice of Dondelume's bride and death
   Soared starward, clear and strong—

" Away, whose Love-wronged heart but loved
   ' Things lovely ' as of yore,
That didst endure, fight and die pure—
   Away now to that shore,
Whose kindred hearts, Love binds — not
   parts—
And passion breaks no more ! "

Narrative Poems

THE RABBI'S PRESENT

A RABBI once, by all admired,
    Received, of high esteem the sign,
From those his goodness thus inspired,
    A present of a cask of wine.

But lo! when soon he came to draw,
    A miracle, in mode as rapid,
But quite unlike what Cana saw,
    Had turned his wine to water vapid.

The Rabbi never knew the cause,
    For miracles are things of mystery,
Tho' some, like this, have had their laws
    Explained from facts of private history.

His friends, whom love did aptly teach,
   Wished all to share the gracious task,
So planned to bring a bottle each,
   And pour their wine in one great cask.

Now one, by chance, thought, "None will
    know,
   And with the wine of all my brothers
One pint of water well may go."
   And so by chance thought all the others !

QUESTIONS

BESIDE a mill, where ran a merry stream,
　A child, there making flower-chains and fun,
Stopped in her play, and with a happy gleam
Asked pretty, prattling things about the stream,—
　Where it arose, and whither it would run;
Then, skipping airily along the theme,
　She asked about the mill and what was done.

An old man answered her who knew the spot,
　But little knew of any place beside.
And he said much to the inquiring dot,
Much that was true, and much more that was not,
　Of stream and mill and things thereto allied;
Then growing garrulous, mixed up the lot,
　And introduced the dim, vast sea beside.

At first the child had listened and been pleased ;
　But, wearied soon, grew still and looked around ;
Then the first moment for escape she seized,
　And, laughing, left the lecture with a bound,
Flew to the things she loved until appeased,
　And heard, with no new joy, the mill's soft
　　sound.

Children are we, who sometimes wondering go,
　With thoughts about life's stream and murmur-
　　ing mill,
To ask those who, we think, perchance might
　　know ;
And find our zest and grip for things they show,
　Now keen, now languid, and now simply nil :
But all their wisdom has an easy flow,
　And on they talk, until they talk us still.
And when set free, to our old haunts we go,
　And hear, with our old ears, Life's murmuring
　　mill.

A SINLESS child—a bright sweet elf of seven ;
　　Looked up, perplexed—a Bible on her knee :
" Mother," she said, " now tell me, what *is* Heaven ;
　　And how will people be ? "

The lady started, ah, what charm was there ;
　　And if 'twas less than lilies can display
'Twas not that she did toil not and give care
　　To be arrayed as they.

" Nay, ask your father, dear."　The father smiled,
　　Then to himself—looking from face to face—
Murmured : " We're told they'll be like you, dear
　　　child,
　　You with her form and grace."

BROKEN JOYS

I HEARD a child go singing down the street :
  Merrily came the trill ;
When suddenly stopped the sound of her little feet.
  And the voice was still.

Some careless curses broke upon her song
  Chilling her with the shock ;
Her joy was dashed, as waves, that ripple along,
  Are dashed upon the rock.

O life ! what music and what Heaven-taught mirth,
  From hearts still pure that flow,
Men kill with sudden frights at this sad earth,
  And never even know !

CARVED in silver, rich and bright,
  In their hallowed niches shining,
With an apostolic light,
  In the world without declining,

Stand the bold apostles all,
  When with sternness puritanic
Cromwell's glance proclaims their fall,
  Riveting the dean with panic.

Asks he pointing with his sword,
  " Who are these ? " the dean replying,
" The apostles of our Lord,
  Ministers all time defying."

" Then," says Cromwell, " sure they should,
  Coined, throughout the world be handed,
Going about and doing good,
  Even as their Lord commanded.'

In the crowded city street,
　Unrewarded and neglected,
Mid the rush of hurrying feet,
　Solitary, sad, dejected,

Stands, with violin in hand,
　One by Fame and Fortune slighted,
One of Orpheus' scattered band,
　Scattered, but in heart united.

Thus depressed he turns away ;
　When a passing stranger lingers,
Begs his violin to play,
　Sways the chords with magic fingers.

30

Then the thrilling tones that rise
   Stop the teeming tide of traffic,
As the genius in disguise
   Sways their souls with sounds seraphic.

And the scorned one, scorned so long,
   Reaps, with gratitude and gladness,
All the harvest that the throng
   Showers in storms of gleeful madness.

Thus sometimes, too, when the bard,
   Silent, sad, is slowly turning
From a world, whose cold regard
   Wears his heart with wasted yearning,

From the realm of kindred souls
   Flies to touch the lips that falter,
Some great spirit with the coals
   Caught from song's immortal altar.

Stands he then aside, retired
   For that voice strong, certain, clear:
Sings he then the songs inspired,
   And the world stands still to hear

A FABLE

ONCE, through the streets of Paradise, was led
   A mortal, burdened but with one command :
Whatever foolish things were done or said,
   To scorn not what he could not understand.

First he beheld two angels with a beam,
   Who bore it crosswise against all they met ;
And spoke not, no, nor smiled, lest he should
   To slight the mandate he did not forget.

Next, with amazement, he could ill surmount,
   He saw a seraph, splashed with shining spray,
Holding a cup that leaked beneath a fount,
   While all the lustrous liquid slipped away.

Amazed, he still was mute in his amaze;
   But when he saw two pairs of horses proud
Straining to draw one car in opposite ways,
   His scorn could bear no more, and cried aloud.

Whereat the angels answered not, but straight
   Hurried to hurl him back into the world;
And so he fell from Heaven; but at the gate
   He turned to see those steeds with wings out-
     furled.

And humbled, as the car rose in the air,
   The mortal owned God's ways are always good,
And that the soul may come to count most fair
   What the poor sense has scorned, misunder-
     stood.

A REBUKE

STRENGTH is shown in sweet persuasions ;
    Fortitude in silent strife ;
Greatness, less on great occasions
    Than in acts of common life.

Histories of the sons of glory,
    Tales that centuries have not hid,
Tell, in larger type the story
    Of the things they daily did

Not in floods or fires or fighting
    Was their greatness, wisdom more ;
'Twas but gleams of chance uplighting
    All their worth concealed before.

When Xanthippe, mad with anger,
  Tried the sage with stormy ways,
He, to shun her wordy clangour,
  Sought the sunshine's cheerful rays.

Madder she that all sedately
  Mused he there and nothing said,
Flung some noisome water straightly
  At the sage's sacred head.

Then said Socrates, the wise one,
  In his wisdom, calmness, wit,
" That, good wife, should not surprise one,
  And the circumstance is fit.

" For 'twere sure no common wonder
  Had so threatening, fierce an hour,
Black with signs of storm and thunder,
  Passed away without a shower."

A GOOD ANSWER

THE deepest truths and the most grand
  Are oftest simply told :
Unspoilt their pearls of perfect beauty stand
  Like gems in pure plain gold :—

A little child untaught, untried
  Of any school of thought,
When asked how many gods there were, replied
  " One God ! " as she'd been taught.

But farther asked how we could know,
  Said of her own wise lore,
" Why, God Himself fills all the world ; and so,
  There is no room for more ! "

"MR. SMITH"

No lineage, and no degree,
   No influential kin or kith,
No prestige, no *bon ton* has he—
   Our Mr. Smith!

Big ears—big feet—a trifle fat!
   His pose grotesque, his walk a waddle!
Meek eyes and lashless! hair quite flat
   On his flat noddle!

He's not a poet nor a wag,
   He's not one scientific notion;
But no spoilt chit or wit can brag
   Of more devotion.

Oh, Mr. Smith, you're " nuts to crack ! "
　　But money ?　Is he rich and thrifty ?
He's but the coat now on his back ;
　　He's right down shifty !

He never worked in all his days,
　　Yet eats and drinks to full satiety ;
And keeps (ah, me ! my blighted ways !)
　　In good society.

Of him no rich and kind papa,
　　No scheming poor mamma afraid is,
He's lots of friends—is loved—yah ! bah!
　　By two sweet ladies !

By two : and one—yes, either now
　　(But for that Smith—ill-fortune take him !)
Might be my bliss, my—oh, their row !
　　Or I would shake him !

Hi ! ho ! my life's a humdrum jog,
　　Its dream dreamed out—its goal a myth ;
And what cares he, that beast—that dog—
　　That four-legged Smith ?

LOVE AT FIRST SIGHT

'Twas the first hush of eventide
   (My time to dream ; and yours nigh to)
The stars were up, though sleepy-eyed,
   When I found you.

And no one seemed to see us, dear,
   (Of course the birds had gone to bed)
And no one seemed to care to hear
   What we two said.

But oh, how we began to talk ;
   And soon I asked : " Would it be right
To take a little lonely walk ? "
   And you said " Quite."

And then ungloved, soft, dimpled, pink,
   Your hand clasped mine (it was not hot)
I asked : " Have we done wrong d'you think ? "
   And you thought " Not ! "

We weren't a most romantic pair :
   I don't think you heaved any sighs ;
But next, I know, your long, loose hair
   Was in my eyes.

Thus on we drifted, more and more,
   Till lovers frank, and—yes—you kissed me !
And oh, the world, well lost before,
   Might now have hissed me.

For you were mine—but oh, how soon
   For golden grain I'd glistening chaff—
You'd flown, coquette ! to hail the moon,
   And dance and laugh.

The spell was broken : but, my dear,
   I'm pleased to think my heart was not ;
And oft in mem'ry's starlight clear
   'Twill haunt that spot.

I've roamed about, and I am such
    As love (and ride off now and then)
But never did I love so much
    A maid—of ten !

LITTLE BEBÉE

(A Recollection of Ouida's "Two Little
Wooden Shoes.")

She sold her flowers in the street,
  A dreaming, gay, untutored child;
Her flowers, her dreams and she were sweet,
  Were sweet and undefiled.

Throughout the glad, bright summer day
  She'd chat and laugh as neighbours passed,
And when eve came would steal to pray
  In the cathedral vast.

Then with light heart and basket light,
  Would seek her home and train her vine,
And tend her flowers, and night by night,
  Lay some on Mary's shrine.

42

She lived alone—had long lived so ;
   Happy, secure, by night and day ;
And little of earth she seemed to know,
   Save she was little *Bebée*.

But now, when she was just sixteen,
   And save for Mary and her flowers,
Had known no love for years, nor seen
   Elate or anguished hours.

There came an artist fair and grand,
   To paint the old cathedral there,
Where little Bebée, bouquets in hand,
   Scented the summer air.

Ah Love ! I will not linger here—
   How first he talked, then day by day
Absorbed her soul, till life seemed drear
   If he once kept away.

I will not speak of those sweet hours
   When Victor took her home at eve—
The pride with which she showed her flowers,
   The flower-like fancies she would weave.

Master alike of vice and art,
  To this sweet, simple child of Day
He seemed a god ; and for her part—
  Why, she was little Bebée !

He had bought many ; but her chaste smiles
  Into his inmost conscience stole ;
Her simple virtue quelled the wiles
  Of his schooled, selfish soul.

He stood amazed, unnerved, o'erthrown,
  Then fled and lied : he'd come again.
Never before had that man known
  Such depth of bliss and pain !

And she, she waited long and wept,
  And hoped and wept and hoped again ;
And read the books he'd given ; and kept
  His memory without stain.

So time passed on, a month, a year!
  Sadder and stranger, day by day,
She would know none, and those most near
  Now scarce knew little *Bebée*.

And then she read by some strange chance,
   Of Victor " known to fame so well,"
" Ill, in the gay bright heart of France,"
   And "poor 'twas sad to tell."

And hope came back, hope leaping high—
   Ill ! poor ! it might be wanting bread ;
She'd nurse him : she would toil, would die,
   To pillow his fair head.

She had no money ; long had her flowers
   Run wild o'er beds she'd ceased to trim—
On foot from Brussels : God ! those hours !
   To Paris and to him !

But on, on, on ; the towns were passed
   (How passed let guardian angels tell)
Paris was gained ; his house at last—
   " Ah me ! should he be well ! "

Up many stairs, through doors that glide,
   Then to a curtained arch, stay ! stay !
No, dazed, she just crept through and cried—
   " 'Tis I, your little Bebée ! "

Ah, shriek, Bebée! would sight had failed
  For evermore, for every face,
If that, or worse than that had veiled
  The picture of that place!

Many bright eyes flashed on *Bebée*;
  But hers called forth that wild alarm,
Who knelt where pale worn Victor lay,
  Wrapt in her dusky arm.

A shriek! a strange sad shriek of woe!
  And then one bound from out that light—
On, on to where the river did flow,
  Like *Lethe* through the night!

But no! they stopped her; and again
  (Let those who will pursue the track)
They brought her home; but it was vain:
  Her mind they brought not back.

And in that cot, o'er-run with flowers,
  The kindly neighbours watched in turn,
While ever through the past dark hours
  Her brain would reel and burn.

Till once, when the tired watcher slept,
　　She wandered forth and sought the mere,
Past Mary's shrine, where she had wept
　　Through that long desolate year :

"Ah! 'tis the Seine!" and she must flee!
　　There, there, the blistering streets she'd trod :
"Mary knows all; she'll speak for me,
　　And I'm so tired, dear God!"

Fragments from Two Hearts

PART FIRST

I.

OF HER HEART—ITS DESIRE.

With Easter guests the house was throng,
  A varied and not small selection :
Folk given up to dance and song,
  To flirting, gossip, introspection ;
Two souls discussed life's right and wrong
  One thought upon the Resurrection.

A maiden young whose face was fair,
  And not less sweet for its strange sadness :
Oft to that old hall's house of prayer,
  She hied her from the scenes of gladness—
So oft alone did she kneel there,
  Her friends called her devotions madness.

Her eyes were beauteous to behold—
  How beauteous when, at Eventide,
In that dim chapel, which the gold
  And rubies of the sunset dyed,
Alone, her fair white hand, she'd fold,
  And pray, " My Lord, make me Thy bride."

Thus ever was the prayer she made ;
  And all who knew her did attest,
One impulse she alone obeyed —
  One pure ambition fired her breast
To live for Christ, till of Death laid
  In virgin white, his bride confessed.

An Anglican, she knew no vow
  Save self-imposed ones.   In devotions
And charity she but sought how
  To flee the world and all its notions—
A saint : one read it on her brow,
  Unrippled of this life's commotions.

And yet, withal, she knew not rest :
  " My Lord," she prayed with burning zeal,

" Show me the path wherein the best
  My hands shall toil, my knees shall kneel,
Where most Thy Peace shall calm my breast,
  Where best thy world-mocked wounds to heal."

II.

OF HIS HEART—ITS CONVICTION.

A poet, or a man whose rhymes
Song deigned to take and sing betimes,
Wearied but wherefore he knew not,
And wanting folk said Heaven knew what,
Was thrown by some sweet chance or power
(Shaped in an April thunder-shower),
In solitude, within the thrall
Of that fair maid, whom in the hall,
He had but seen as one who sees,
A fitful moonbeam through the trees.
Now, flooded of her soul's strange light,
He thrilled to song; and sang that night :—

I know that naught save love can satisfy,
  And can love do it?

For many a prize I've learned and ceased to sigh ;
To many a goal I've pressed and passed it by.
    To bless nor rue it.
Life on the whole seems not so much awry ;
    But through and through it,
I know that naught save love can satisfy,
    And can love do it ?

III.

OF HER HEART—ITS WANDERINGS.

She wandered forth perplexed and sad,
    And sought the night to soothe her pain—
To lose dreams which had made her glad,
    To dream of loss as future gain—
"He's fair and good, but oh !" she cried,
"I thought to be but Heaven's bride !"
A voice replied, "Or maid or wife,
Seek thou the narrow path of life !"

Then down dim aisles, through arches hoar,
    Where the Past reigned and ghosts had part,
Ghost-like she passed, and knelt before
    The Altar of the Sacred Heart.

"Oh, I would leave the world," she said,
"And live as one man counteth dead!"
And the voice answered, "Child, arise,
Not hence thy pathway to the skies!"

She sought the calm, eternal stars,
    And saw Orion, like a cross
Built up of God with golden bars,
    Pure of man's guilt, and greed, and dross.
"O God, I would rise light and free,
And climb the stars unto Thy knee!"
And the voice answered, "Child, away!
Thy strength shall be as is thy day."

She passed into the thronging street,
    And saw the flare and heard the din,
And watched the seething currents meet
    Of shame and woe and want and sin.
"Oh, I would lose myself," she cried,
"To save souls 'whelmed in this dark tide!"
Then the voice said, "Were it not best
To wholly fill one human breast?"

She gained the garden gate to see
   The man o'er whom she'd cast a spell :
"Oh, why—why must we part," said she,
   "How should I—could I—say farewell?"
Her tears then blurred with blood-red bars,
The street, the altar, and the stars ;
And the voice said, "In calm or strife,
Should not love prove the gate of Life?"

IV.

OF HIS HEART—ITS PURSUIT.

Ho! the land of pines and mountains,
Flashing snow-peaks, foaming fountains.

Vineyards green and meadows golden,
Blue-sky-kissed, of blue lakes holden

Forest-clouded, flower-bespangled,
Glacier-gemmed and torrent-tangled ;

Violet-clotted, crimson-streaked,
Azure-bathed and snow-white-peaked !

Land whose garb, as she can show it,
Painter never caught or poet.

Green gown, olive—emerald-shaded,
Pearl-embroidered, amber-braided,

Frieze-grey-hooded, purple-caped,
White-cloud-frilled and black-cloud-craped !

Land that seeks for man, by day,
All earth's dyes to make her gay ;

And for God's pure eyes, each night,
Kneels in changeless, spotless white !

Busy land—towns hive-like, crowded ;
Lonely land—homes terror-shrouded ;

Jovial streets where gay wheels go ;
Pine-paths dim to pathless snow.

Merry land—bedizened, dancing ;
Trance-still land—stern, heavenward-glancing.

Sweet-voiced land—chimes, cowbells ringing,
Horns resounding, woodmen singing,

Echo-shunned and song-bird-banned :
Pulseless, ghostless, silent land !

Land most wondrous ; now to be
Thrice more wonderful to me !

Thither in pursuit I fly,
Of the maid for whom I'd die.

Maid that holds my spell-bound will,
Stranger, fairer, purer still !

V.

OF HER HEART—OVERTAKEN.

Why must my soul be dark to-night
  With such a starry sky ?
When all this world smiles pure and bright,
  Why should I wish to die ?

Ye starry skies, be angels' eyes—
　And each white peak a nun !
Black mountain nigh be Sinai.
　What have I said or done?

I kiss my cross, my vow record,
　Still but Heaven's bride to be ;
But oh, were Heaven now mine, dear Lord,
　Or e'er my Heaven is he.

Yea, could my soul but quit its clay,
　As that pearled purple breath
Now quits this hushed, white corpse of day,
　How beautiful were death !

No pledge he asks and no caress ;
　He follows when I fly ;
Would Heaven make him love me less,
　Or love me that I die !

VI.

OF HIS HEART—ITS PLEA.

You say my words are empty things ;
　And that is wholly true.
They're but the flash of thoughts, whose wings
　Soar on to Heaven and you.

You say I do not know you yet;
   And that I fear is so.
The heights of Life which you forget,
   I've not yet come to know.

Yet you have said our souls nigh touch;
   And should I dream to say,
That all your words are wise, but such
   As leave me room to pray?

No, where were flow'rs of earth uncloyed?
   Or saints where sin mayn't be?
How were the stars without the void?
   What wouldst thou, lacking me?

VII.

OF HIS HEART AND HERS—CONFLICT.

"Truly thou dost believe in God."

   "Aye, child, in God, myself and thee."

   "Wilt thou thus always answer me?—
Myself and thee? How soon the sod,
Once breathing dust, where I have trod,

Will be the dust *thou* knowst as me.
Put me aside ; and speak of God,
Whose breath, figured in flesh, are we,
As I had passed, as I were dead,
Or else as if thou ne'er hadst known me."

"That cannot I whose heart and head
Have best found God as thou hast shown me :—
He gave me thee to lift, to throne me
High in a heaven of love and wonder,
Wherefrom, entranced, I hear his tread,
And feel him round me, o'er me, under."

"Nay ! for we soon might drift asunder :
I need not thee that God be read ;
Nor need'st thou me ; if I had fled,
How should'st thou more or less believe?"

"Neither : God speaks to them that grieve,
Loud as to them whose joy is vast—
Louder : Who hears the sunbeams weave
The forest? but we hear the blast :
God speaks, through hope, through doubt, through fear,
    through fear,
To all things so that all things hear.

Yea, I believe in God most high.
Had joy, had love, hadst *thou* gone by,
Thus then as now, and in the past,
Had Life grown one long tangled lie,
And truth here, past all finding out,
Wearied and wishful but to die,
Too tired to hope, too sick to doubt,
Too numbed to care, or how, or why—
I yet should know God ruled on high."

"How couldst thou? What would bring
    him nigh?
Oh, how thou dost assault my soul!
Without a church, without His word,
I had no will—a fluttering bird
Buffeted 'twixt the earth and sky,
Without a guide, without a goal,
I should pant out this life and die.
How can'st thou live without a creed?
Alas! how different thou and I!
And what of Him by whom we're freed—
Who for our sins did weep and bleed?
When by the world, and wrong enticed,

Where dost thou flee? Where dost thou hide?
In anguish, where wilt thou abide?
Dying? save in that riven side?
Tell me, what thinkest thou of Christ?"

"He is our brother, and God's son."

"Yea, God, and with the Father one."

"Child, hush thee: Angels have appeared,
    To strengthen mortals when they feared;
To hold them when they would have run!
    To break their prison bars and lead them,
    To bid them do what Heaven may need
        them;
But never underneath the sun
    Have I yet read, or heard, or thought of,
Either in times of peace or schism,
    Or urged by love, or duty taught of,
An angel with a catechism.
Thou art my angel winning-wise:
Thou holdest me: thy Heaven-filled eyes
    Chain me in Heaven's vicinity.
    Thou liftest me: thy strong faith flings
    Round me its glad, swift, cleaving wings,

So that out of myself I rise ;
    Are not thy sweet rebukes and prayers
    My stumbling feet's illumined stairs,
From earth up to God's purest skies ?
Would'st turn my soul's inquisitor,
Who came its Heaven-franked visitor ? "

"Whence comes thy strength ?   For me to live
    Is to *believe* in heart and head.
My strength He—only He—can give ;
    To know I live, and shall not pine,
It cometh only with that bread,—
    His body broken for my sake,
    Which, with His blessèd blood made wine,
Hunger to stay, and thirst to slake,
Meek on my trembling knees I take,
    And feed, and feel His life in mine.
But ah—Nay, I will hold my peace ;
For I too am the sport of doubt,
    Of questionings that will not cease.
Should not I first the beam cast out
    From mine own eye e'er motes from
      thine ? "

"Of doubt?   Thou? surely, if there be
One blessĕd soul free from that thrall,
Child-like, secure, believing all—
On whom God's perfect peace doth fall,
'Tis thou : dove-like it rests on thee."

"Peace?   Nay—for ever in my breast
Throbbeth the anguish of unrest ;
My Faith brings all but peace to me."

"What ails thy soul?"

"A weary quest :
Her home on earth where she may rest :
The Rock secure, the seal unbroken ;
Authority's unquestioned token,
    To me to thee, to age to youth,
Once only, and for ever spoken :—
    My Christ's commands—Eternal Truth
Thou knowest how I love to pray,
Where the dear Virgin hath her shrine ;
The maid of whom our Lord was born,
The mother from whom He was torn,
What should she to our Lord not say

For every woman's heart and mine?
Woman most loved, and most forlorn,
How should she throned in Heaven not pray
For women who would grow divine?"

"Thou art a Papist, child, to-day:
Confess it: Would'st thou like confession?
For *me*—No! There I draw the line!
I loathe it, and 'tis my impression———"

"Oh, hush thee, hush! I loathe it too—
Humiliation's gallèd wine;
But if God wills it—if 'tis true———"

"True? I should say 'twas hell's device;
And Satan's most esteemed possession———"

"Stay! stay! now thou hast stabbed we
      twice;
And thou art rash: suffice! suffice!
I know not what to say or do;
But this I know: nor fire, nor ice,
Nor earth, nor hell, nor priest, nor *you*,
Shall make me swerve when God shall guide me;
And He *will* guide and help me too—

Lead me, and hold, and fold, and hide me—
Oh, were I this wild conflict through!"

"Child, God would give thee peace alway,
Deep as *my* peace with thee beside me ;
Be as thou art : do good and pray ;
So truth shall come, and we——"

"Nay!   Nay!
In Heaven there will be peace ; and then,
If thou shouldst seek me yet again—"

"Nay, thou shalt find thy peace below ;
And be *my* peace !"

"I fear me, no.
For ever since I was a child
I have had conflicts strange and wild ;
And also—ever and again—
One rare bright vision.   Dost thou smile?"

"Nay, not at thee, thou hast no guile.
Tell me, what vision chased thy pain?"

" Jesus with children at His knee.
'Twas always thus. 'Tis now, as when
I was a child, and thought good men
Must all His loved disciples be."

" They are : Hold there, and anchor fast. '

" In childhood's dreams when childhood's
      past ?
Nay ; but I see them disagree,
    Wrangle and rail on either hand,
Priests, preachers, and—good men like thee.
Yet doth that beauteous vision last,
Jesus with children at His knee.
Ah, could there be one faithful band,
One fold, one voice through every land—
That voice : ' Let children come to Me.'
And child-like, simple, faithful, pure,
From schism, variance, strife secure,
Christians *did* come, this world throughout,
One Church, one Faith—and just one doubt."

" What doubt, strange child ? "

" That they were meet
To name His name, and kiss His feet."

"An angel !   And His child indeed !
That dream is a child-angel's dream ;
Yet purer daily grows Life's stream ;
Truth brighter shines—-and what is doubt,
But feeling for the things we need ?—
Now Faith when one her eyes puts out ;
Now Faith born blind that gropes about,
And stumbles till the light commences ?
Truth (which is light) must be our cry--
Light (whence is growth) till by and by,
The soul's light *may* eclipse the senses'."

"Yea, Truth is light—the Truth confessed
Of angels, and once given to men.
Give me that light the Truth dispenses,
And hide all others from my ken—
Beacons that but add doubt to doubt,
Lead us and lure us on and out,
Farther and farther from that rest,
Which the poor, groping, staggering senses
Seek, to assuage the unquiet breast.
And now perchance, now, but for thee,
This day I had fulfilled my quest—

This restless heart at rest might be
In the great calm of that great sea,
Rome's——"

   "What, child? Thou wouldst build thy nest
In that old tottering tower of Rome?
     Nay, but thy soul's of stronger wing:
'Twill soar above St. Peter's dome!
     Seek we the Truth to make us free!"

   "Ah, yes, thy conscience is thy king:
     Mine a plagued pilot still at sea.
I only know my Father's hand
Will take mine, ere the dark's complete—
Will guide me o'er Life's shifting sand,
Wherein would sink my wandering feet;
But thee, I never more may meet,
Save where there shall no temple stand,
There, in that far-off golden street,
When we have said good-bye——"

   "Good-bye?
Oh, never, never! blest, or banned,
At variance, or with eye to eye—
If hours flash on o'er golden sand,

Or time a black, slow conduit rolls,
Let us together fall or stand.
Let us in patience win our souls.
Bid me forget bliss e'er, was nigh—
Remember thou shalt ne'er be mine;
Say to me hopes shall have no bloom,
Nor aches a balm, nor fears a tomb,
Only say not that thou wilt fly!
Bid me be mute, and ask no sign;
Only forbid me not the room
To merge my destinies in thine.
Be naught to me, so thou be nigh!
Say aught so thou say not 'good-bye!'"

"Oh, cease: thy pleadings shame my heart;
What canst *thou* love in such as I?
Had I been other than I can be!——"

"Not by one thought; but for my par
Would I were all thou wouldst have man be,
If only——"

"Hush; see in the sky,
How the faint stars grow strong and bright,
As the blurred earth fades out of sight:—

Love is not lost, nor ever can be ;
It hath but seemed to fade and die.
'Tis hid.   Then death, which is God's hand
Casting its shadow where we stand,
Maketh it Heaven as it makes night !
Love to love's home for ever flies,
As stars crowd to the starry skies :—
Back to God's breast the soul has sped,
Naught, naught save one blurred day is *dead.*"

VIII.

OF HIS HEART AND HERS, AS THEY AFFECTED OTHERS.

" In health or sickness, calm or strife,
   Love is to men the wine of life.

" By his own door each grows his vine,
   Presses the grapes, and drinks the wine.

" All grown alike—with joy, tears, toil !
   But the wine varies with the soil.

" And some need much—some little use,
   But somehow, like the widow's cruse,

" It serves most men to Life's last drowth,
  When the tired hand can't reach the mouth."

" But there are hearts, I think you'll own,
  That sicken on the wine they've grown.

" And Ahab-like begin to pine ;
  And plot to steal their neighbours vine."

  " And yet again, Love dreams and dares,
Ventures afar, and homeward bears,

" Trophies for eyes to gloat upon,
  The fabled grapes of Echelon."

  " As for those grapes—Nay, broach the keg,
And drink, each man, down to his peg,

" Of his own vintage, his own share,
  The good old cheap *vin ordinaire.*

" Grapes for the gods—Nay, food for rats ;
  They rot before they reach the vats."

" Nay, they are pressed betimes I know,
Who drained *one* goblet long ago :

" Ruby-red, as the sun's eclipse,
That goblet as it touched my lips;

" Dashed from me, into darkness thrust,
Dazzling, dissolving, starry dust ! "

" Simply, you mean that draught divine,
Proved for *your* head too strong a wine ? "

" Perhaps ! 'Twas young ; but *now* I think——"

" If the chance came, you'd like a drink ? "

" The wine of youth (which turns it mad)
Manhood wants when it can't be had !

" Take this young poet's hot mad chase :
He's love-drunk.   *There's* a drunkard's case

" Foiled, checked, he thinks that girl divine,
Full to the lips of Youth's new wine.

"Ten years hence he'll mark Aphrodite."

"So will his wife and call her flighty."

"'Fair creature,' to himself he'll mutter:
His heart may warm ; but it *won't* flutter."

"Aye those two *are* a love-mad couple ;
God wot he's strong, and she is supple.

"Like reeds which to the river thrill.
She bends herself unto his will.

"And reed-like, as the river-grass
She bends herself to let him pass."

"To my idea, no fool is he.
None of your flounced, frilled dolls for me—

"Your dimpled, dancing, parrot-clever,
Little cheap wound-up joys-for-ever."

"No, nor your maids with stockings blue,
And spectacles of a kindred hue.

"It makes me blush that coloured stocking;
  White, shown to the garter, weren't half so
    shocking."

  "Aye, and her sister a trifle older
Who bares, or shapely or not, her shoulder,

"Only to show the wretch she stirs
  She'll wrest the world from *his* to *hers*."

  "Oh yes, he's wise and lucky!—In fine
He's loved by a maid that is half divine.

"By day he draws, and she yields her hand,
  To drift by night to the Angels' land.

  "And what will get her, and whose she'll be,
God wot, it would be a fine thing to see,

"A cloistered soul with no cloister's taint,
  Or a married miracle-witnessed saint!"

  "That's very good, if you don't mistake her;
That is, if she's half the saint you make her.

" But these are Religion's golden days ;
   And truly her ways are winning ways.

" O, Israel, how fair thy tents ;
   Thy vestures and flowers and songs and scents.

" Thy chiefs are humble, and their humility
   Bringeth them titles of nobility.

" Thou biddest the poor sit down at ease ;
   While the rich serve them on bended knees.

" Thou seekest the lowly—with anxiety—
   And sayest ' Sit here '—in the best society.

" Thou vauntest the cross—of pain and passion ?
   Or of cult and clique for thy dames of fashion ?

" For those who would climb up the mountain
      delectable—
Stand where men envy them, honoured, *respect-*
   able,

" One day in thy courts is better—a lot—
   Than a thousand outside—with the wicked or
   not.

" For a damsel who cannot laugh and spin
　When she's conquered her own and the family's
　　　sin,

" And the poor and sick, by her father's door,
　Are poor and needy and sick no more,

" What crown has Life that she'd look upon it
　By the crown so *chic* of a church-trimmed
　　　bonnet ?

" For who is the rival, keenest, truest,
　To the richest dame or of blood the bluest,

" But the Church's own little Marjory Daw
　Who sleeps (with the blind up) on her straw ?

" The former may queen it, in London mobs,
　O'er statesmen and poets and lords and snobs :

" But the latter presides at more famous dinners,
　Who paradeth the slums to sit down with sinners."

" Thank you, as one in a kind of way
A servant, and proud of his church to-day.

" I think your chaff flung far and free
   For the winds to winnow, my friend—not me,

" Might prove to contain a seed or so
   Of notions one might permit to grow.

" *My* church will survive *your* sneers.   What next? "

                    ɔ

         " Well ! *I* would preach from another text :—

" O Israel, how fair thy tents,
   And filthy the lucre that pays the rents.

" For the rich who rough-shod, at Mammon's
      beck,
   Over Humanity's prostrate neck,

" Have ridden hard for the devil's fold
   Are thy chief seats, that are bought and sold.

" The seats of the mighty, who should be saints,
   But are walking purses and masks and paints.

" *They* honour thy gates, have their garments kissed ;
   They head thy scroll—a subscription list.

"Thou drivest them in from the hedge and ditch,
  Nolens volens, the rabble rich.

"But whether in wedding garb or not
  They may sup at ease if they pay their shot.

"Thy pillars once were the poor and needy,
  Now thy pride and prop are the rich and greedy.

"Thou flatterest them, till the best are sick
  To stand in the shoes thou bidst men lick.

"Another turn in affairs polemic,
  Thou'lt lose the rich of an epidemic,

"Were it not truer to say, and better,
  That they'll lose *thee*, like a broken fetter.

"How shalt thou save them, that own'st them thy
    saver?
  What shalt thou give them, that beggest their
    favour?

"Thou hast taught them gold is the Church's
    rock ;
  They're the salt of the earth and feed the flock ;

" Their treasure's in Heaven ; and as they die,
  They canter in squads thro' the needle's eye."

" Be that as it may.   But you'll allow
Christians ne'er lived like Christ as now !

" Never since Christian Times' first tick
  So fed the hungry, healed the sick,

" So probed this great world's wondrous heart,
  Leapt with its joy, shrank with its smart,

" So preached to men man's brotherhood,
  Like to their Lord, in doing good."

" Aye, that is true : now when they say
To wretched sinners, ' Let us pray '

' Be they reclaimed or still transgressing,
  'Tis firstly when one asks a blessing.

" The fire to come has given way
  Unto the fire men want to-day.

" Over the holy inquisition
  Sits haply now some mild physician,

" Debating for the body's sake,
  Not if they'll send men to the stake,

" But whether ('tis a wiser plan)
  They'll send a steak unto the man.

" Yea, crowds may spread their cloaks and say,
  ' Hosanna to the Church this day.' "

  " Hosanna ! All you've said is true :
Honour unto whom honour's due.

" But does not Science cry and Song,
  ' The Poor shall not be with us long ' ?

" If that's to make this bad world blest,
  What do the saints more than the rest ?

" 'They give to get ' an urgent claim,'
  But do not publicans the same ?

" Indeed save for the herdmen's smocks
  'Twere hard to choose between the flocks.

" Sheep have no sheepish bleat or coat ;
   Dumb to the shearer goes the goat.

" For bargaining folk and most litigious,
   Commend me to the folks religious.

" Unworldly-world, left, in the lurch :
   Folks oftest left without a church !

" Take those two lovers : there's a riddle,
   They match—

" Match like the cat and fiddle.

" One is as pious as the other !

" Then Piety can make a pother,

" Oh, *they're* half cranky.

" Or half divine ?

" Their tether's a limit.   Pay out the line.

" Whirled on in all the ways of wonder,
   Now drawing nigh, now swept asunder.

" A moth enamoured of a feather,
 Let them fly up to Heaven together.

" For good or ill, for joy or dearth,
 They'll soon drop somewhere, earth to earth ! "

" She to a convent ; he old Harry ! "

" Please God they might grow sane and marry."

" What is the girl ? A Sister ? No ! "

" They're anxious to enlist her, tho'! "

" Is she a Papist ? "

" No, not yet ! "

" Nor ever will be."

" Will you bet ? "

 " Not I, she may turn Turk or Jew,
For aught I care ; and where's *his* pew ? "

" He's no religion ! "

"So you're told :
He's not of any branded fold."

" That is to say, where 'er he goes,
The devil leads him by the nose ! "

" He leads him oft then where you'll say,
His majesty has lost his way :

" To your own church ; and tho' I own
He does stray farther from his throne.

" Satan might seem a trifle odd
As verger in *that* House of God ! "

" Goes he to hear the holy mass ? "

" Not he ; he goes to see—— '

" Alas ! "

" You've said the word : Her satellite,
He flutters round that radiant sprite.

" While moth-like she performs her capers,
Drawn to the light of saints and—tapers."

" Nay, nay, 'twere a mean sin to jest
  When youth's hot heart can find no rest,

" Because, forsooth, nor hope nor harm
  Stirs the old heart's chill, stagnant calm.

" I do remember me, this day,
  The light that fell across my way ;

" The angel walking by my side,
  The tongues of fire that prophesied ! "

" And did those tongues, that angel, say,
  Show thee more excellent a way ? "

" Plainly, where wise age gropes ; and youth
  Runs with its radiant lamp of truth !

" O, flickering light, O voices dim,
  On that choked path from youth to Him.

" O, pledged but pride-scorned peace, which He,
  Not as the world, had given me—

" Not as the world, marred, insecure,
  But sweet, inviolable, pure !

" Drawn of those hands, which, round me flung,
  My sins have pierced, my slights have stung,

" Pressed to that heart, which broken, smarted
  To pillow, then, the broken-hearted,

" Rocked on that breast, Love's plumbless sea,
  My lovelessness made moan for me,

" My soul had lain stilled, satisfied,
  Hid in His life for me that died."

"Peace to thy soul, for sure God's Peace
Seeks him who so from self would cease ! "

" Aye, but the seed that should now be sheaves,
Where the cold rain drips on the rotting leaves."

" Peace, aged soul, God takes thy tears ;
And counts them as sheaves for the barren years—

Yea sheaves : Let despair not thy Faith destroy,
Which the reapers, the angels, bear up with joy."

IX.

OF HER HEART—ABNEGATION.

She looked upon the pale cold sky,
  On the warm, green, life-giving earth ;
She looked on love's dim by and by,
  On the glad day that gave it birth.

She thought on maids whose love can die,
  She thought upon the saints long dead ;
She only gave one weary sigh,
  And this is what that one sigh said :

Your eyes are full of love, my sweet,
  And love it comes from Heaven, I know ;
And Heaven itself is but replete
  With love such as here learns to grow.

"Oh, you, my love, Heaven, all combined,
  Could but my life with your life blend,
Entwine, dissolve, be lost ; and find
  Its own sure, sweet, unconscious end.'

A voice replied, " Child, hush thy fears,
　Die but thou thus ; doubt would be dead " ;
She only answered with her tears,
　And this is what those hot tears said :

" Leave my lone heart and let it ache ;
　There is an ache that would be worse.
Should I thus die, and dead, then wake
　To know I'd clasped him to his curse ! "

X.

OF HIS HEART—WISDOM.

Forget the joy, forgive the pain,
　Which I have brought to thee ;
Forgive I made thee forge my chain,
　Forget I am not free.

Remember thou didst make me glad,
　And brighten all my lot ;
That I shall ever now be sad,
　Do thou remember not.

Forgive I made thee, sorely driven,
 Show me thy love supprest ;
Forget none now, in torrents, given,
 Could ever fill my breast.

Remember that my fate was such,
 Thy spell I could not flee ;
Forgive that I have loved too much,
 Forget thou lovest me.

Forgive ! forget ! and for my part,
 I'll keep thee in thy shrine ;
And ne'er, ne'er weight thee with my heart,
 Till thou wouldst give me thine.

XI.

OF THE HEARTS OF CHILDREN AS THEY AFFECTED HERS.

"Dear child, why hast thou left thy play?
What ails thee that thou art not gay?

"Wherefore unto my chamber hie?
Why kiss me thus?   Why dost thou cry?"

CÉCILE.

Because—oh, Mademoiselle, you're good,
And John and I've quarrelled in the wood.

He said that m'sieur but for thee
Had shown him the nest in the linden tree.

MLLE. (*aside*).

Aye, *but for me*—'tis always so—
His heart had been blithe as John's, I trow.

CÉCILE.

So he said this and I said that,
Till he called me a little papish cat.

Why dost thou hide from m'sieur thus,
When it makes it so sad and dull for us?

He loves thee with all his heart and mind;
And is he not handsome and strong and kind?

MLLE. (*aside*).

Oh, hush, be still, my sweet wee friend:
Must thou, too, learn my heart to rend

CÉCILE.

Wilt thou not seek him now with me,
And take him to John by the linden tree?

MLLE. (*aside*).

Seek him, my child?—could I be as thou,
My heart had rest from all seeking now.
(*Aloud.*) When he called thee a little papish cat?

CÉCILE.

Oh, he loves me—so I'll forgive him that.

And he says, if I keep true to him,
And they wall me up in a convent grim,

He'll seek and find me, and wait and wait
Till he's got an army to force the gate.

MLLE.

Brave Jean!
    (*Aside.*) (Would walled-in souls that moan
Dwelt but in convents made of stone).

And what says Father Merle of John?

CÉCILE.

He'll be very sorry when he has gone.

And John likes him—he will sit on his knee,
And coax him to catch and to tickle me.

He has read all the books that ever were written;
But he's just like John when they teaze the kitten.

He can talk of each country beneath the sky,
Of the stars, and of heroes and saints gone by—

And he plays at croquet with John and me;
But come: John's gone to the linden tree.

MLLE. (*aside*).

Oh, how thy beautiful, young heart,
Unconscious, plays the woman's part.

Let John arise; naught else 'twill see,
And curés and saints have ceased to be.

(*Aloud.*) I cannot go—not now, my child ;
Stay thou with me ; the night grows wild.

The clouds are black—and hark ! the rain,
Like rubble thrown at the window pane !

CÉCILE (*at the window, gaily*).

Oh, Mademoiselle, the sky's like ink ;
And listen—'twill rain again, I think.

MLLE.

Good gracious, child, what's that ?

CÉCILE.
                O, hide me ;
'Tis John : he's coming ; he has spied me.

Here? there ! No—lying on the bed,
As stiff and still as I were dead.

JOHN.

Bon soir, Madame. Where's——? Oh, I see !

Cécile.

I'm dead, and you weren't kind to me ;

But I forgave you, when I died ;
And soon you'll find another bride—

A Protestant, rich, proud, and fat,
Who'll scratch you when you call her cat.

John.

Cécile, get up !

Cécile.

Then beg my pardon !
Where's Monsieur ?

John.

Moping in the garden.

Cécile

Poor Monsieur, all alone, forsaken ;
I'll go—oh no, I must be taken,

All white and stiff—dear Monsieur'd miss me ;
"Sweet child," he'd say, and stoop and kiss me.

Then, John, you'd say, while all were crying,
I pled for him when I was dying,

And Mademoiselle and he would wed;
And *you*——

JOHN.

Cécile, don't—*don't* be dead!
Get up; it's wrong; it makes me queer!

CÉCILE.

I won't; death's nice!

MLLE.

My dear! my dear!

Jump up. How can you do so?—fie!

CÉCILE.

To play at death!—'tis wicked? Why?

They act it oft; and stories; look:
There's some one dead in every book.

And no one cares—dear John, don't cry!

JOHN.

I—I should care, if you *did* die.

CÉCILE.

Well, then, I won't—see! I'm not dead;
So let us play at getting wed.

This is the altar, there the priest—

JOHN.

But where—where is the wedding feast?

CÉCILE.

And flow'rs for me, and grapes for you——

(*A flash of lightning and loud thunder.*)
Oh, Mademoiselle, is this wrong too?

MLLE.

No, child
CÉCILE.

Oh dear, I often wonder
Why God should like to talk in thunder.

I never know what things He's saying;
But mother, now, I know is praying.

And you—you have no kind of fear—
John! John! come from the window, dear.

JOHN

Why?   Thunder's naught to men and boys;
That isn't God; it's only noise!

MLLE.

Nay, dear, the lightning sometimes kills,
But ever only as God wills.

JOHN.

Why, then, we need not fear being hit;
And I'm not frightened—not a bit.

My father knows; he says 'tis gas;
And if I fear it I'm an ass.

First comes the flash; 'tis naught—zigzag;
Then clap!—a big, burst paper bag.

(Close to the window.)

My father knows, Cécile; so see:
"Thunder and lightning fall on me!"

*(A vivid flash and loud report, at which Cécile
screams.)*

You see; my father knows; but hark,
How the waters rush, and it's nearly dark.

I wonder what poor M'sieur's doing;
He did not see a storm was brewing.

And ere I came to seek you here,
He thought of roaming abroad, I fear.

CÉCILE.

Oh, Mademoiselle, if he has gone!
How cold your hand, and your face—how wan!

JOHN.

Dear Mademoiselle, you need not mind,
For Monsieur loves the rain and wind.

He loves to climb some steep ascent
When the pines creak and the rocks are rent.

He'll think no more of the thunder's crack
Than of twigs he snaps on the mountain track.

To-night his face was like a stone,
And he wished to think and to be alone

He was not cross, but he bade me go,
While he walked moodily to and fro.

I think, when I am big like him,
I shall be often fierce and grim.

He looks so grand, and he doesn't care
What people say, nor how they stare.

They say that he's like a king in chains,
And his heart is eaten with fiery pains.

But that is rubbish; they do not know!
He's only vexed that you shun him so.

So he shuns *them* : he's proud, you see;
But he's always gentle and kind to me.

8

MLLE. (*aside*).

Oh, hush thee, hush, my gentle child—
What seeks he in this night so wild?

CÉCILE.

Say, Mademoiselle, now did you make
The sign of the cross for Monsieur's sake?

He may be safe in the little mill—
That is, if he'd time to cross the rill;

But the rains soon make it a raging tide;
And the plank is railless, and swings beside;

And rubble and rocks roll down that glen—
Jesus and Maria shield him then!

MLLE.

Oh, hush thee, child; God holds the thunder,

CÉCILE.

But the earth and rocks that it tears asunder,

And the crashing pines; if the swoll'n rill—
I fear—why, Mademoiselle, you're ill!

*   *   *

See, Mademoiselle, a gleam of light!

MLLE. (aside).

Ah, God, for one in my long, black night!

CÉCILE.

What did you say, dear Mademoiselle?

MLLE.

Oh, nothing, my child; I'm nearly well!

CÉCILE.

Oh, look, the sunshine on the trees!
Mother is rising from her knees!

JOHN.

And Monsieur will be walking quick,
Slashing the pine cones with his stick!

MLLE.

Then go, dear children; make them gay;
I now would be alone

CÉCILE.

To pray?

MLLE.

Perhaps.   For that I sought my room.

CÉCILE.

Dear Mademoiselle, do you *love* gloom?

MLLE.

No, I love *you*, so kiss me quick,
Then run.   Here, John, don't leave your stick.

Take it to Monsieur—go to meet him;
And if he's wet, be sure you beat him.

(*Aside.*) Would I could meet him blythe as you.

JOHN.

I will, and say *you* told me to.

MLLE.

You rogue, don't say we feared the weather;
To-morrow we'll romp out together!

JOHN.

And Monsieur too?

CÉCILE.

Yes, if he's good!

JOHN.

We'll all play *cache cache* in the wood!

Cécile, come quick; it's all blue sky!

CÉCILE.

Dear Mademoiselle, goodbye! goodbye

MLLE.

My pet, you'll squeeze me quite in two;
You don't love me *so* much!

CÉCILE.
                    I do;

I love you with a love that—oh!
No one but John and Monsieur know!

You'll pray for me and John and mother?—
That we may always have each other!

And never quarrel when we vary!
Do *you* pray to our Mother Mary?

MLLE.

Yes, child.

CÉCILE.

How nice!   Dear John, don't fuss—
Then, Mademoiseile, you're one of *us?*

MLLE.

Not quite.

CÉCILE.

Why not?   Don't you confess?

MLLE.

No.

CÉCILE.

But you will—you *must!*—oh, yes!

And Father Merle—you'll like him so—
He'll tell you all you need to know.

Mother confesses when she's sad,
And others when—when they've been bad.

And you—oh, yes—you'll seek him next,
Dear Mademoiselle, when you're perplexed.

We often wonder—John and I—
Why you, sometimes, so strangely sigh,

And sit and think and knit your brow—
Tell him your troubles!   Will you now?

MLLE.

Dear child, I often talk with Father——

CÉCILE.

And he's helped you?

MLLE. (*aside*).
Nay, hindered, rather.

CÉCILE.

I'm sure he will; I always know
When mother's been—he soothes her so.

And oh, she is so light and gay
And kind after confession day.

It's like this sunshine after thunder;
What he has said I often wonder—

He is so very wise you see—

MLLE. (*aside*).

(But *I* know what he said to me.)

CÉCILE.

She always comes when she's confessed
And snatches me unto her breast,

And says—I know well what 'twill be :
Nothing shall come 'twixt her and me.

MLLE. (*aside*).

Alas, alas !   And I've but been
To learn all things would come between—

That earth must pass and Heav'n grow dim
Ere that Church gave me peace—and him.

CECILE.

Dear Mademoiselle, you do not speak,
And the colour has faded from your cheek ;

And, there ! you are knitting your brows again,
And you've all gone back into gloom and pain.

Mlle.

Then kiss me and away, my dear—
John's a sad heretic, I fear.

Cecile.

Indeed he is, but—why, he's gone !
Oh, I never think of such things with John !

Do you with Monsieur ?   Let me go—
They are different—they—they are men, you
    know !

And what does it matter ?   They're good.   Good-
    bye—
Perhaps they'll be Catholics ere they die.

They'll have to be then.   But I declare—
They're men, and they love us, and I don't care !

Alone.

A man and he loves me !   Aye, pure and rare
Is the love that he gives.   And I don't care.

And I don't care if I live to rue,
And curse my fetters ?   I do, I do !

"And what does it matter?" oh child most wise!
He may be a Catholic ere he dies.

A man and a true one! Oh, I·do care:
Who bade them bind me? how do they dare?

What do they know? how can they see?
What is The Council of Trent to me?

What is the voice of the Church and what—
What am I?—I where he is not?

A Catholic when he dies?—ah, no;
Nor now, nor ever; but "let me go——"

For I won't care—not for canon or creed;
Not for pope nor priest, nor for all their seed.

A man, and I love him, and he loves *me*;
And they, they would bind me and scourge; but
    see:

Torn from my soul, their gyves I toss,
And I break my bonds as I break this cross!

(She snaps in two her little crucifix, then pauses
motionless and silent.)

Broken—my Saviour on the tree !
'Tis wood, 'tis naught, and I am free.

I've done but as thousands have done before.
Peace !—peace !

("Nay, that will return no more ! ")

Who speaks?   There never *was* peace for me ;
Papist or Protestant, bound or free.

(She puts the two pieces of the crucifix together.)

Now never care nor prayer nor pain
Can make this just the same again !

How many times on bended knee
Have I clasped this—but I am free !

("Aye, free, but thus forever broken ;
Keep it as of thyself the token."

"Thy broken, useless self, to be
His curse who'd give his life for thee.")

I give him mine !

("Nay, but the pieces :
The substance when the soul deceases.")

Silence !   He and his God to guide me,
What should I lack that he could chide me ?

("Thyself !   With that behind thee left,
Should he not be of all bereft ?

" He would not have thee break thy cross ;
He never called *thy* symbols dross !")

'Tis they have brought my soul to this :
The Church's blessing, or his kiss?

(" What church ? ")

I know not.   Cease !   No more !
My soul, my heart, my brain is sore :—

Madness's millstones round and round !
Have they not broken—crushed me—ground ?

What Church ?   No Church !   And if no rest,
Rapture—on my beloved's breast !

XII.

OF HER HEART—SURRENDER.

The moonbeans wanton and shimmer
   Where lovers walk lost in the vines.
With laughs come the flutter and glimmer
   From them that the dance entwines.
Day dies and his red stains grow dimmer ;
   My love cometh down from the pines.

Heart be at rest from thy roaming,
   Soul be at peace at thy bars ;
Ye have writhed in your torment, to foaming ;
   Ye have torn me—behold now the scars !
But he comes, my beloved, with the gloaming,
   And round and about him the stars !

Sleep, sleep then the fears that would hold me,
   A truce to the saints and their rest !
Hushed all be the voices that told me
   To seek him in realms of the blest ;
Now, now my beloved would enfold me—
   How shall I not lean on his breast ?

Yea, leaning on him let me wander ;
   For why should God drive me alone ?
How point him to crowns that are yonder ;
   When here, in my heart is his throne,
And his house ? When he knocks should I ponder
   On mansions and crowns for my own ?

He comes—doubt away, for I list not !
   But give me his breast for my balms !
Peace ? When, if with him now I tryst not,
   Whose step all my terror becalms ?
What to me Heaven's kiss of him kissed not ?
   My love ! Let me fall in his arms !

XIII.

OF HIS HEART WITH HERS—TRIUMPH.

Fair as the flush on the mountain ;
 Supple and straight as the pine ;
Buoyant and bright as the fountain ;
 Clinging and sweet as the vine :—
Playful as fountain with mountain
  She that is mine !

Blithe as the cow-bells in May-time ;
 Peer of the chamois for pride ;
Torrent-tossed happy by day-time ;
 Calm with the stars on the tide :—
Mated as haytime to Maytime
  I by her side !

XIV.

OF HIS HEART—FOREBODINGS.

With dance and song, amid the gay,
 I too lost care ;
My heart was like the blossom-crowded May,
 For thou wast there.

The dance, the music, and the mirth
　　Went whirling on ;
My heart was like the dead-leaf soddened earth,
　　For thou hadst gone.

The music-whirled, flower-given throng
　　Will ever be ;
But life would lose its bloom, and time its song,
　　If I lost thee.

XV.

OF HIS HEART—SHADOWS.

Clear lies the moon-touched tranquil lake,
　　Clear rise the mountains high ;
The fields, the vines all one pale image make
　　Of the sweet day gone by.

And in my heart black shadows fall,
　　And the cold moonbeams play ;
And clear and calm and silent, I recall
　　Its warm, sweet pulsing day—

Aye calm as moonlight on a tomb,
　　And murmurless as night :
Better thine image mirrored in my gloom
　　Than all new things of light !

XVI.

OF HIS HEART, AS HE FIGURED ITS FATE
AND HERS.

The summer brought the burning hours,
 The autumn brings the rain ;
And loves that loitered o'er the flowers,
 Now hasten with the grain,
To find their rest in cots and towers,
 And cabins by the main.
   And I'd the flowers ;
   But wintry hours
Nor home nor rest bring me :—
My love she lives upon the rocks, and I live on
  the sea.

I see her when the breakers roar,
 As white as they with woe ;
And when I toss in peril sore
 She wanders to and fro ;
And sadly, from a sunlit shore,
 She'll sing the songs I know !
   Oh love will lie
   Or love will fly ;
9

But not for her and me :—
My love she will not quit the rocks, and I can't
    quit the sea.

And none will ever know our past,
    For it has left us dumb ;
And now each day is like the last,
    There are no days to come :
The sea, the rocks, and the round vast
    They make our earthly sum !
        For man and ghost
        They shun this coast
(Why I mayn't tell to thee),
Where she, my love, lives on the rocks, and I live
    on the sea.

Wail, wearied winds that cannot cease !
    Moan, unadvancing waves !
Whisper, ye depths of unfound peace !
    Babble, ye vacant caves :—
Moan for the dead that cannot cease,
    The living in their graves !
        Aye moan and roar,
        "No more ! no more !" :—

My love that loveth me,
She'll dash herself down from the rocks, when I'm
    drowned in the sea !

XVII.

OF HER HEART—ITS VERDICT.

Once more, but once, beneath thy spell—
One look, one word :—that word " farewell.

Only farewell, with no disguise,
No smiles untrue, no laughing lies.

Farewell ; I cannot say it boldly ;
I will not say it curtly, coldly.

With broken voice, with breaking heart,
Farewell, because God bids us part.

Farewell, to leave thee free behind me,
To go where thou shalt never find me.

To be what thou shalt never know :—
Farewell, because I love thee so !—

Because, where'er my soul's dark cell,
'Twill be less dark dost thou fare well.

XVIII.

OF HIS HEART—ITS DOOM.

And this is love? her love and mine,
  Dost hear my heart? 'tis love :
The one thing on this earth divine,
  The only one above !

Thou hast been loved, art and shalt be,
  And so shall she—as much ;
And when the sky shall clasp the sea,
  Thy love and hers shall touch !

'Tis love ; and love o'er all shall reign !
  Aye ! that now well know I—
Shall fill my soul and heart and brain,
  This love which is goodbye !

XIX.

OF HIS HEART—ALONE.

Unto the bee the honey cell ;
   The butterfly the bloom ;
Unto the thrush the dewy dell ;
   The bat and me our gloom !

Unto the cavalier romance ;
   The soldier honour's goal ;
Unto the gamester dazzling chance ;
   The monk his quiet soul.

And unto me the paths I know,
   That lead not anywhere—
The goalless, soulless to and fro,
   With the dread doom I bear.

For pangs men bear, the balm of Time ;
   Hemlock for those that won't ;
Burdens for all who live to climb ;
   Bubbles for those who don't.

And unto me the void and chill
  Where my heart used to beat—
Burdens that were as bubbles till
  They melted at my feet.

Unto the loved, their lovers' eyes ;
  Idyls for those loved not ;
Stars for whose loves are in the skies ;
  Graves for the loves forgot.

And unto me, most loved of men,
  And loving more than they,
Nor eyes, nor stars, nor grave—for then
  This death had died away.

XX.

OF HIS HEART—ITS GHOSTS.

That was a flower, when she was here ;
  Those leaves—brown, gold, and red :—
She said they never died, poor dear—
  Were only put to bed.

The autumn crocus ! millions, wild :
    She stooped to touch one purple cup ;
Then laughed, and said they'd souls, sweet
      child,
    And would not pluck them up.

That white-sailed boat, the broad, blue lake,
    The purple shadows there.
The snow-touched sky—they used to make
    A dream of earth and air.

Yon calm red-clotted, snow-barred height
    Was Christ's dead, blood-stained brow ;
"Tis but a common Alpine sight—
    A thing for tourists now !

They call it a strange rapturous sight :
    "Tis not !   It *used* to be !
And then they say I'm mad, and light
    Is darkness unto me.

"Tis they are mad—the chattering daws :
    I know things when they're seen ;
Paints make not rapturous things by laws,
    As blue and yellow, green.

They say the sunset skies now make
  Rivers of divers wines—
Millions of rose leaves flush the lake,
  And fire-brands flick the pines !

They're mad, or seem so unto me,
  I know the tints things *had ;*
That flesh-flaked pearl was then, sweet girl—
  And some one called *her* mad.

Those flesh-flaked filmy falling streaks
  Were angels' arms at dyeing time ;
She said we'd see their eyes and cheeks
  But for those crimson bars of crime.

Now they are gone the angels' dyes ;
  Madmen, 'tis vapour all !
Why do ye stare into the skies ?
  I wish that they *could* fall !

There *is* no sound of birds that sing ;
  No scents, nor sunny hours ;
No green earth floors the sky's blue ring,
  There are no stars nor flowers.

The sun? there *is* no sun—'tis set !
  The world ?   What's that to me?
One round, vast blank where I regret
  The world that used to be !

XXI.

OF HIS HEART—ITS COUNSELLORS.

" Soul, take thine ease ; eat, drink in peace ;
  Because to-night thy life shall cease—

" To-night !   No morn for thee shall break ;
  Therefore unto the darkness wake.

" Arise and shine ; this is *thy* light :—
  Up, and make merry with the night ! "

So spake a voice within his heart ;
But the man answered—' Fool, depart.'

" For I shall neither fight nor flee ;
  Saints would not cross themselves for thee ! "

Straight came another voice and said,
" Poor wretch, 'twere well if thou wert dead."

"Yea," said the man, with heavy sigh,
"Dead as my heart, whose grave am I."

"Nay," spake the cold, clear voice again,
"Dead things have not that living pain."

"Then kill it—kill *me*, where I stand;
I would not crouch or raise my hand!"

"Then raise thy finger only—so!
Death waits on thee, thy slave, not foe."

"Nay, get thee gone! I understand;
I knew a man oft brave and grand,

"And yet withal—cursed with a trace
Of weakness foreign to his race.

"He raised *his* hand, a reckless one:
A smile, a flash, a thud; twas done.

"His face was calm, but what know I?
Thus to quit life, is that to die?"

"Yea, soldiers die thus by the million ;
　And dance with Death—a gay cotillion !"

"'Tis false ; each bayonet bites by reason
　They fall as leaves fall—*in their season.*—

"Tread the red wine-press out and *die*—
　Some happy that death passed not by !

"Thus would I take Death's *given* kiss—
　Dreams, sleep, oblivion, aught but this.

"I would behold her white, fair face,
　I would be crushed in her embrace ! "

"Why, then, she stoopeth o'er thee now,
　Her lips nigh touch thy burning brow.

"Her hair is falling in thine eyes ;
　Clasp they new love before she flies.

"Thou movest not, ah coward, now ;
　Thou lov'st not Death nor such as thou ! "

"Traitor, thou know'st it would not be ;
Liar, thou know'st she seeks not me ;

"What though I love her more than breath,
'Twere hell, not Love, would ravish death."

A silence fell ; his eyes grew dim ;
A soft voice then thus spake with him :—

"Aye, weep, nor heed the sophist's sneers :—
Wisdom will come not for thy tears :

"Should the sweet dews make moist the skies ?
Nay ; but we weep *because* we're wise."

Unanswered, that calm spirit fled ;
Then one as with a clarion said :—

"Seed of the wind ; bloom of an hour !
The tickled earth for a tarnished flow'r !

"Only the plough-share, only pain
For the bread of life, for the market grain ? "

" Cease !   Blatant platitudes of Truth ;
   Precepts dinned at me from my youth !

" I know thee, face, and voice, and vestures,
   Thy pulpit phlegm, thy platform gestures,

" Telling the happy—but in vain,
   How good is want, how grand is pain.

" I know the things that thou would'st say ;
   They're truths ; so take them hence away—

" Where ears can hear, where eyes can see—
   Anywhere, anywhere far from me.

" I can but see one vanished face,
   That lingers ghost-like in its place.

" I can but hear one voice that rings
   Like dying throbs from broken strings ;

" And feel—nay feeling all are o'er,
   Save hearts can feel they'll feel no more '

" Of course they can," a new voice cried,
" And feel next day how feelings lied.

" But dead to touch, and sight, and sound,
I'll take thee, come, on thine own ground.

" Thou canst *remember*—good and bad ;
As yet *thou* art not wholly mad."

" I ?   She is less, save madness taints
The whole community of saints ! "

" She's acted as one mad to thee."

" I've said so : May God pardon me

" For I did sin ; there are some souls
Who plume their wings for such high goals,

" We lose them, as they lose earth's leaven ;
They're mad *to us*, as we to Heaven."

" True ! still for all that touches thee—
What thou can'st feel, or hear, or see.

" 'Mid sane folk here, as sane things go,
  Did she act sanely ?—yes or no ? "

" Sanely ? Oh, to the devil, thou,
  That forgest bands to burst my brow.

" Does the child deem its mother sane
  Who flings it in the foaming main,

" With the life-belt about its neck,
  When the flames lick the doomèd deck ? "

" Ah ! pretty ! then thou dost agree
  She has the fire and thou the sea ?

" She loves thee, spite of Heaven's frown,
  Loves thee more than a martyr's crown,

" But not enough to dare to see
  The fire she feeds consuming thee.

" Thou know'st or shouldst know there are born
  Souls that in Heaven are writ ' forlorn.' "

" Never ! I know not ; nor does man
  Mortal 'neath an immortal bann ! "

" How wise again, and over wise ;
  The bond's for earth—forged in the skies.

" Break it ; men can break all God's laws ;
  What comes ? Death with wide-open jaws ?

" Nay, Time's wrong tick, a trivial jar,
  The unfelt swerving of a star.

" Then wider sweeps——"

" Oh yes that clever :—
  One wrong thing runs amuck forever.

" And so it may !—what odds, you ranter,
  If right ones have as fine a canter ? "

" Aye, jest it proves thee better—sprightly ;
  Thou'lt soon talk sense—perhaps politely.

" Wisdom is food and wit is season ;
  But Folly's fattening spiced with reason."

" Sober or sprightly, fool art thou
  To talk of centuries from now."

" I flatter thee : What's time ?—Well here,
  A breath—some millions to the year !

" But in the time that follows death
  Some million years may make a breath.

" And even here the hours, you'll find,
  Can only measure dust, not mind.

" That house, we say, that hand, that flower
  Will last an age, a year, an hour.

" A long night's rest ? an hour of lust ?
  How long were that ? Time measures dust !

" An age in heaven ; an hour in hell,
  How long were that ? Time cannot tell.

" Nor can mind measure time ; as soon
  Should the month measure out the moon.

" God measures time ; and now I ween
  No spirit knows how much there's been."

" Aye that *is* true : had that old clock
  Gone with my heart from its first shock,

" Ticked with its throbs and worn its chain
  As I have worn my heart and brain,

" Wheeled its wheels with my hopes and fears,
  "Twould stand now with the rust of years."

" Yet none the less, and after all,
  There stands God's dial on the wall :

" It metes to men (take hour for hour,
  And shine for shine and shower for shower),

" Who live to see the west go grey,
  About the same, and same-sized day.

" You look at it, as minutes fly,
    You with your neighbours, eye-to-eye.

" And hourly, you all remark
    'The line creeps on, 'twill soon be dark ! '

" And when your eyes grow dim you pray,
    And turn you to the wall, and say,

" What you would do (but don't, alack !)
    If God would let that line go back.

" There you're at one : that shows *your* reason,
    Worms of one soil, moths of one season !

" And when your neighbour's mind is sound
    Where is his treasure ?—in the ground.

" His lips? upon some long-life phial ;
    His eyes ?—Fixed on that fearsome dial.

" But she ?——"

" What, are we there again ?
    Would'st hint with flattery she's insane ? "

" She is not sane to such as thou ;
   Look in her eyes, look on her brow.

" Look—thou art privileged—in her heart ;
   What is the compass, what the chart ? "

" She's mad then ; and Heaven's brightest spark
   Glimmers where madness mocks the dark."

" Nay, she is only mad to thee,
   Whose wisdom angels may not see.

" Hast thou not said so ? Be content :
   Recall *thy* madness, and repent.

" Endure slowly to forget—"

" Begone ! "

         " Adieu ! Thy task is set."

" Forget ? "—

A bantering voice then said,
" Never ! who e'er forgets their dead ? "

" What, yet more comforters? begone !
    I'm worn : but if thou wilt, rant on.

" 'Tis all the same."

        " Nay, now not quite ;
    But I might call another night.

" I saw your light in going to sup ;
    And just looked in to cheer you up."

" *To cheer me up ?* To lighten lead ?
    Let me alone ! My head ! my head !

" What seekest thou ? "

        " Thy good.   Don't doubt it :
    Thy head ?   Don't think so much about it '

" And for thy heart, poor fickle toy,
  'Twill serve *thy* time for grief and joy.

" To-morrow's bubbles will divert it
  As yesterday's; and will not hurt it."

  I fear no hurt—if aught could calm it."

" Then Life's no ill 'gainst which to arm it !

" And thou canst pass thy few short days
  Secure from shock, or dream, or craze,

" Sleep, wake and walk, and take thy victuals ;
  Now work a bit, now play at skittles."

    " Play ?—"

" Certainly, play after school,
  The game that's on—cards, rackets, pool

    " Leave me !"

"I'm off: but don't pretend
Saddles and guns have had an end!"

"Fool!"

"What, shall those be too forgot?
Do naught, then: just hang on and rot—

"Leaf-like to dangle, fade, and fall;
'Twon't be for long: death comes to all.

"Leaf-like, ye flutter to the sod;
And then—Ah, he begins to nod!"

"I'm wearied out—but who art thou,
That dost not leave me, even now?"

"Who? Thy best friend!—Ah, now he's still!
Poor soul, I have thee at my will.

"Poor tired, tortured one, thy breast
At length is calm; thou art at rest!

" So rest ; then wake and seek thy pain ;
  Rave, and I soon will come again—

" Come, and still come, till by and by,
  One comes more powerful than I—

" One who comes not to such as thou ;
  For *I* can smooth thy knotted brow,

" Thy wild heart hush, thy hot brain steep :—
  I am God's angel, callèd sleep ! "

XXII.

OF HIS HEART—A CRY OF SORROW.

The crimson flush has fled the snowy mountain,
  The ruby clasp has fallen from its zone,
The boughs are black that veiled the flashing foun-
    tain,
  The silver steps are tarnished up the Rhone,
The girdling vineyards tattered, stripped, forsaken,
  Cling to lake Leman, shivering dim and grey ;
And lone and chilled, forsaken, sorrow-taken,
  I wander with my heart where we were gay.

The sweet *luzerne*, the *sainfoin* and the hay-time,
 They'll come again, with the green, tender
   vines ;
The lake will shimmer both by night and daytime,
 The ruby shafts will fall athwart the pines,
The sun will flash on leaf-entangled fountains,
 The Rhone will shine a thread of silver sea,
The old tint glint on fountains, forests, mountains ;
 But never, never, never more for me !

XXIII.

OF HIS HEART—A CRY OF DESPAIR.

  The arrow has failed ;
   The bow is unstrung ;
  The summer has paled ;
   Songs cease that were sung.

  My heart is aweary ;
   And worn is my brain ;
  The daylight dawns dreary ;
   Night adds to my pain.

Quit me, faint muttering,
Impotent Breath ;
Kiss me, nigh-fluttering,
Sweet and strong Death !

XXIV.

OF HIS HEART—APATHY.

'Tis Christmastide, and in my breast
I hide the ache and pain ;
But bid me not be merry, lest
You bid me be insane !

The old year's dead.   Let the wreaths fall,
I'll rave not by his bier ;
But save you'd mock my dead heart's pall,
Wish me no glad New Year.

Wish—cold beneath this winter's snows,
Or warm at spring's warm breast—
Wish me the blessedness of those,
Dead or alive, at rest.

There was a time—how long ago—
    They say 'tis just a year,
But dials ne'er were made to show
    The lifetime of a tear.

They only show how near is night,
    And death—to other men :
No wheels can calculate the flight
    Betwixt one's now and then.

There was a time—how long ago!—
    When Spring, a child in glee,
Hot-cheeked came romping thro' the snow,
    To make a child of me.

I loved to hear the linnet sing
    Upon the first green bough,
And think joy was a natural thing :
    Would I could think so now !

The linnet, he's a winning note ;
   I heard him sing to-day,
And watched his rapturous little throat
   Shake the white hawthorn spray.

I looked and listened to the end,
   And half forgot 'twas I ;
Nor knew that I had found a friend,
   Till friend-like he'd gone by.

Then, on old days I found how deep
   He'd dipped in chat with me ;
Anon I mused and fell asleep
   In listening to a bee.

I had wooed sleep—had wished to fling
   All thought in Lethe's stream ;
But sure, Heaven sent some better thing,
   It brought so bright a dream.

She came, her eyes haunts of that light
   And love not man's to be—
Cells whence some hiding angel might
   Have looked at earth—and me.

She spoke—how did my wild heart leap,
  That asked so oft to break :
" Who giveth His belovèd sleep,
  Giveth them to awake,"

"To sleep aweary ; waken strong—
  Sleep fettered ; waken free ! "
I woke : 'twas but the linnet's song,
  The humming of the bee.

" He giveth His belovèd sleep : "
  Aye that perchance might be ;
God help me, then, more to love men.
  Till He shall so love me.

 END OF PART I

Fragments From Two Hearts.

PART SECOND.

(*AFTER AN INTERVAL OF YEARS.*)

I.

OF HER HEART—ITS QUEST.

At a church door—beneath the stars—
  Where the cold slabs their secrets kept,
A woman peered through iron bars,
    And moaned and wept.

A passing spirit took the guise
  Of woman's want and shame forlorn,
And asked with hollow, burning eyes,
    "Whom dost thou mourn?

"Thy child? thy husband dost thou seek?
   Thy lover lost in love's first youth?"
The woman said in accents meek,
     "I seek the Truth."

"The Truth?" The spirit laughed and fled.
   " Fool that I was to pity *thee ;*
The Truth is known but to the dead ;
     What's Truth to *me ?* "

Then down the dark, foul city street
   The wailing, drooping spirit passed ;
The woman, touched with pity sweet,
     Followed her fast.

All through the great, grim town that night,
   She followed, praying her to rest—
Through darkness and through flaring light,
     Now east, now west—

Past homes of pleasure and of care—-
   Where joy was rife, where anguish deep,
Where women woke to pray, and where
     Men laughed asleep—

On, on, until, at morning-tide,
 She clasped her—kissed her haggard cheek ;
" Poor, weary wandering one," she cried,
 " What dost *thou* seek ? "

The spirit flung his figments by—
 All radiant from God's starry throne,
" An angel of the Truth am I,
 And seek mine own ;

" Come, rest ! He finds not Truth who delves
 Through darksome ways to dim, far goals.
But Truth finds them who lose themselves
 In others' souls."

II.

OF HER HEART—ITS FINDINGS.

Was it a dream—but coloured thought ?
Was there no angel, vision, naught,

That through those sad streets I should roam
Till I had tracked that lost one home ?

Till in that *home* I then should faint
And *they* should call me " blessèd saint " ?

They, by whose side, O Holy Saviour,
We *all* were saints in our behaviour?

But if no angel's thought or care
Took shape and lived one moment there,

Whence and what was she, in that place,
That had an angel's voice and face ?—

Caught me when falling, and caressed ?
Blessed me so that I have been blessed ?

It matters not—what fell that day :
Since then a year has passed away!

A year in which I naught have seen
But sin, by which most sins look clean—

Sin like a worm within the flower,
Sin like a fire within the tower,

Sin—like a torn, crushed, crawling thing
That once flashed fair on sunlit wing,

Sin—like a snowdrop painted scarlet—
When innocence puts on the harlot !

Sin—like the stage flare aping day,
The innocence that harlots play !

Sin sleeping, struggling, anguished, gay—
Sin ! sin !—and some sin washed away !

Yea, thus a year has passed ; and I,
With some sin's death begin to die.

In those dead souls, which Life now choose,
I *do* begin myself to lose—

Yea lose myself ; and if, forsooth,
I find no more than erst the Truth,

I find at least, when they find life,
Respite from that soul-strangling strife.

I have known rest—aye, rest and peace,
When I have seen *their* wanderings cease.

And when I've seen my Saviour's feet
Washed by *their* tears—those tears made meet,

Inhaling as from Paradise
That out-poured ointment without price,

Then found my soul, without alloy,
The angels' fragrant food of joy.

O blessèd toil, O welcome sphere,
That now has filled one sweet calm year—

A year of rest, by labour bought
Out of the restless mill of thought—

A mill which, whirring faster, louder,
By now had ground my mind to powder,

Had not that mill's last falling sands
Taught me to feed it with my *hands !*

My hands, frail hands, what can they do,
Saviour, whose hands my sins nailed through ?

What can they find—what hold for Thee,
Whose hands so long have holden me?

My hands, my frail, weak woman's hands,
I offer them as one who stands,

And would be hired to do Thy will,
Master that callest labourers still.

Take them! an offering poor and mean,
Take them : at least my *hands* are clean.

Guide them, Thou, and they shall not fail ;
Hold them, Thou, and they shall not quail.

Busy them, Thou, where they should be ;
Then thought and will shall cease for me.

Empty or full, but let them find
Thee needing them, sick, wretched, blind.

Let them be shackled or be free,
Groping—so that they grope for Thee.

Snatch them from all I would, so I
Thy hand-clasp feel when night is nigh.

Lose them for naught, that in Life's wreck
I find them round my Saviour's neck.

III.

OF THE SACRED HEART, AS REVEALED TO HERS.

The moonlight fell across her bed,
On her calm face—calm as the dead—

On her soft hair and her fair brow,
Fair as the blue-veined marble now.

From untold hours with sufferers spent,
Her hour had come to be content.

Her worn hands clasped—her work laid down
Woven her life's wild olive crown !

As thus she lay in languor deep,
An angel slid into her sleep,

And moved as 'twere Bethesda's pool,
Pure, passionless and deep and cool,

Life's long-watched waters, for her soul,
That she might bathe there and be whole.

She dreamed ; and evermore, I wis,
Knew Heaven sent her that dream.—"Twas this :—

A woman, with a burden dreary,
In the great city fell a-weary.

Upon the ground her load she laid,
And on a step sat down and prayed.

Straight came a child unto her knee :
'What ails thee, mother?" "I am tired," said
    she.

"Then come with me; my father's home
Is not far hence—where dost though roam?"

"Roam, child.   Bless thy pure heart of pity ;
I roam all ways through this black city !"

" Then thou art poor as well as sick ?
My father feeds the poor—come quick."

" Nay, child, I've gold enough this day;
Though much I've lost—some given away."

" Thou livest thus from choice ?   I doubt it ;
But come : Father would hear about it !"

She smiled : " Thy father's hands, sweet boy,
Won't long be left without employ ;

" For seeking woe here, seems to me
    Seeking salt-water in the sea :

" I'm tired."

" Then come," he pleaded still,
" I'll bear thy burden up the hill."

" Thou, child ? "

" Then half."

" 'Tis not a feather."
And so they laughed and went together.

So pleasing was the boy's gay prattle,
Unseen the crowd, unheard the rattle.

The woman passed through many a street,
Scarce knowing she had moved her feet—

Until, without the smoke-filmed town,
By a grand gate they sat them down.

" Is this thy father's house ? " she cried.
" Not yet.   This is where I reside."

The woman looked—then laughed for joy :
" Thou strange, sweet mischief-loving boy ! "

" Nay, I am gay "—here he laughed too—
" But what I say is always true."

She looked again, through branches bare,
At the far mansion vast and fair.

" Here live I with some hundred others,
Like me—my sisters and my brothers."

"Oh yes," she mused, " I see the dome ;
This is the Little Children's Home."

"Yes 'tis our home and we want you
To come and be our mother—do !

"You'd love us, and we you—don't doubt ;
I *know* that, and you'll find it out."

The woman looked in his sweet eyes
With more of gladness than surprise ;

So did his child-like, strong faith hold her,
They seemed quite wise—the things he told her.

And ever as he pictured more
Her life and his beyond that door,

More seemed it beautiful and meet
That there she thus sat at his feet.

" Ah yes," she cried at length, "indeed
That is the life that I *would* lead.

" Could I my life's task re-begin,
  Set free from this sad fight with sin : "

" Then did'st thou "—asked he with a smile—
  Fighting sin, find it *not* so vile ? "

" Child ! " here she clasped him in dismay,
" Viler than any words could say ! "

" Then 'tis that there—round that black steeple,
  Mid all the wants of all those people,

" Children to thee seem of less worth—
  As thou dost see more of God's earth ? "

" My gentle boy, what dost thou say ?
  Nay, and a million times nay ! nay

" Of all now left—not hid above,
  It is but children I can *love*—

" Love wholly—just as I love thee,
  For what thou art—not mightest be—

" Wast or wilt be, when all is done—
   Love as the sunflower loves the sun ! "

" Yes, thus do we love.   Tell me, pray,
   Could one love in another way ? "

" *We* can't.   So do I now love you—
   Because—because *I have to do*."

She caught and clasped him to her breast :
" Wise child !   That is Love's only test."

Then did his wondrous eyes so shine
It seemed as they had grown divine.

Trembling to loose him, or to hold,
She looked down on his hair of gold ;

And lo, a sunbeam falling now,
Brought him the nimbus for his brow.

" Who art thou ?   Speak ! "—-her heart throbbed
   wild ;
He answered meek, " God's little child :

" Tell me, wilt thou stay here or go ;
   Wilt thou take care of me, or no ? "

" I will, tho' all the world said ' nay,'
Thy wants shall be my care alway."

" And of my sister and my brother ? "
" Yea, of them all—I'll be their mother ! "

Then throbbed her heart with rapture wild
But she dared look not on that child.

Feeling that still his form she pressed
She knew 'twas but her own full breast.

Lost in that bliss—all still, trance-wise,
She waited mute, with closèd eyes.

Then came a voice of sweet accord :
" Woman ! " she turned and said " My Lord " :

Awe, wonder fled.   There was but place
For peace, deep peace, where smiled that face :

"'Thy need hath drawn me from above —
That Jesus thou dost following love."

" My Lord," all fearlessly she cried,
" 'Tis thou hast loved ; I have but tried."

" Nay," said He, " thou hast loved and fed,
Clad me and pillowed my sick head."

" I wearied of it, Lord, forgive —
Wearied, and wished *my* life to live ! "

" Nay, when the days most wearied thee,
Then didst thou weary most for me."

" Here came I but of joy beguiled : "
" Then had I *all* thy heart my child."

" I promised me to quit all care ; "
" For thou hadst learned *my* yoke to bear."

" I would not lose myself for men ; "
" For thou hadst lost thee wholly then."

" Dear Lord "—But more she could not speak ;
The happy tears ran down her cheek.

The vision passed, but from its place
Rare lustre rained upon her face.

She woke : with sunshine and wild bloom
Children and God had filled her room.

'Twas Heaven still, or if 'twas less,
After that rapture in excess,

It was enough—it did suffice :
She was with Him in Paradise.

IV.

OF THE HEART OF THE ALL-WISE AS HE PERCEIVED IT.

A man walked through the city street
With haggard face and bleeding feet.

Begging, he fed men from the sack
He carried on his coatless back.

Begging, to give the sick and sad,
He had spent all he was and had.

Now at death's door, from his bent back
He took and gazed upon his sack—

He prized it : 'Twas to him the sign
That he had sought the life divine.

Then " Friend " to a sick man, said he,
" Sell it : thy need constraineth me."

The sick man, bending from his years,
Looked at him thro' a film of tears.

" Need ? Thou'st thy sack ; I still have shoes,
God wot there's not much room to choose.

" But till thy lean bowed form came by,
Methought Earth's veriest scare was I.

" Why thoughtest to prolong my days ?
Dost *thou* love life ? Dost love men's ways ?

" Here sit thee down, rest there thy head,
  While I go beg or steal *thee* bread.

       *   *   *   *

" What ? Better for that wine and meat ?
  Could'st limp the length of half a street ?

" Then I'd seek means wherewith to try
  To get thee to the wood close by.

" There I've a hut hewn in the stone ;
  There twenty years I've lived alone.

" To-day alone through all that time
  My feet have touched the city's slime.

" They say I hate men and their touch ;
  And faith, 'twere hard to love them much.

" Thou smilest ? Here ! give me thy sack :
  I like thee—get thee on my back.

" I'm not by half the age I look ;
  And crippled, I can leap a brook."

              *   *   *

The man sat smiling at his sack
Beside the hermit's faggot stack.

Kissed into sleep by God's sweet air,
He knew not how he'd journeyed there

"Now," said the hermit, "tell to me
What *is* that thing upon thy knee?—

"That raggèd, torn, gold-broidered thing
Thou hugg'st as it had graced a king?"

The sick man answered with a smile :
"This sack is self's last lure and wile.

"Its age, its holes, its every stain
Tell me I have not lived in vain.

"Had'st thou but taken that and fled,
Then thou had'st left me free—and dead."

"It once had words on : tell them me ;
For they're nigh gone—poor soul, like thee.

" The words ? " the sick man said, " thus ran :
   God loveth him who loveth man.

" *Where sore hearts throb and sad eyes weep,*
   Watch thou, and I will give thee sleep.

" Nay !   Think !   Thy memory is not good,
   Should God not calm me in this wood ?

" Where the kine low and the lambs leap,
   Methinks He'd likelier give *thee* sleep."

The sick man looked on the green sod :
   " 'Twere hard here not to *think of* God.

" But where such balms my senses steep
   Sound to the world's sobs I should sleep."

" Perhaps thou wouldst sleep wisely then ;
   Hast thou borne such great gifts to men ? "

" I have done naught "—he spoke with tears—
" Save to grow old in all but years."

" Dost oftener then God's works adore ?
   Dost understand thy Maker more ? "

" Nay.   But who made me breathing dust
   Made me to wonder and to trust."

" Aye, but He oft makes me be merry—
   Pleased as a blackbird with a cherry.

" And e'en strong angels—more's the pity—
   Grow sick there, in that filthy city.

" The busiest of them mounts for rest
   To God's star-crowded, flower-filled breast."

" Then, who," the sick man meekly said,
" Shall heal the sick and hide the dead ?—

" Snatch the despairer's poisoned cup ;
   Clothe shame, and give the outcast sup ?—

" Lighten, if only by a hair,
   The load of human pain and care ?"

The hermit gave a kindly look ;
"Faith, now thou talkest like a book.

" Here, come !" he seized a half-charred brand—
" Write on my wall there, something grand.

. " I doubt if God used thee so much
To find and heal things with thy *touch*."

"Alas, no !   'Tis a memory sore ;
I oftest knocked at the wrong door."

" Not so to-day !   This no false call :
Write something on my bare stone wall—

" Something that would have stayed *my* tears,
Something to help one twenty years."

He took the charcoal in his hand,
And smiled and murmured "something grand !"

"Once I could write—aye, burning pages,
But I've had no new thought for ages."

" Then try an old one—have no fears :
  Thy best are not of recent years."

"I can't."   He laid the charcoal down,
  Glanced at his sack, and gave a frown.

" Friend, God's good gifts—excepting pain—
  He gives and takes not back again.

" I'll stir the fire "—His voice was sweet—
  "'Thou'lt write to-morrow.   Warm thy feet.

" Dost know I half believe this sack
  Was made for some one else's back ?

"Something's gone wrong, whate'er it be
  The sack, the motto or in thee.

" There's been—aye, that is very clear,
  Some sad misfit for many a year.

" Didst ever ask thy heart—' Do I
  Feed others that myself may die ?' "

" Yea," said the man, and hung his head,
" 'That's been my wish—that I were dead."

" And so to serve thy moment's need,
  Thou wouldst the starry worlds made speed ?

" Dost think one only has to die
  To patch up all amiss gone by ?

" That there 'twill be enough to *know*
  Why things here did not smoothly go ?

" What hast *thou* borne, not borne of old ?
  Lost more than wife, child, friends, and gold ?"

  The man winced as with sudden pain,
  Then picked the charcoal up again.

" I *could* write now—if 'twere the time,
  The last thoughts that I cast in rhyme.

" 'Tis nothing clever nor artistic ;
  'Tis sad ; and sadly egoistic."

" Nay, if thyself thou dost impart,
   Thou givest food unto my heart.

" The egoist—the bore is he
   Who fattens (publicly) on *me*.

" He takes my time, my thoughts, my sense ;
   And gives—when he gives aught—offence—

" Spends all of mine that he *can* spend ;
   And hoards his mean self to the end."

   Forgetting then to forget self,
   The man wrote neath the hermit's shelf—

" I fear 'tis poor, sad stuff," he said ;
   The hermit raised his eyes and read :—

I tread the noisy ways of men,
   And lose me in their woe,
That I may find there, now and then,
   The joys of long ago.

I seek old age and ease its cares,
   And sometimes steal its pain,
That it may sometimes, unawares,
   Give me my youth again.

I prop the pain-racked dying head,
  And night-long watches keep ;
And then sometimes the happy dead
  Come to me in my sleep.

Betimes the white flowers in my hand
  In streets no flowers know,
Show me a tranquil, tuneful land
  Of vines, and pines, and snow.

And when some child has kissed my cheek,
  Borne through the trampling tide,
She comes of whom I may not speak,
  And wantons at my side.

And once in fever's raging glow
  I neared a crimson strand ;
And she stood there, in robes or snow,
  To take me by the hand.

But no ! the crimson flood flowed back,
  And Heaven fled from my ken ;
Once more I sought, with my old sack
  The soiled, sad ways of men.

And here a flower, a crust I give,
   There steal an ache, a sigh,
Helping, by straws, the race to live,
   While it helps me to die.

  The hermit rose. "My friend," said he,
"Thou stirrest up God's gift in me :

"Here, toss me thy old broidered sack ;
   I too possess the scribbler's knack.

"Where sore hearts throb—which side was't on ?
   Try something new : That motto's gone.

"It would have suited one I found
   The other night on holy ground.

"She prayed for truth, and smote her breast,
   Poor soul ! I *lired* her into rest.

"All through the city's roar and light——"
"What ?" said the man—"the other night ?

"Thou saidst for twenty years complete
   The city had not soiled thy feet."

" Nor has it ! Hist ! was that the cock ?
 Time, man ? Dost see I have no clock ?

" That night was twenty years to her ;
 Thou art a hundred—I'll aver.

" But change thy rags and scrape thy face,
 And men will say, ' Youth flies apace ! '

" Now quick ! the gorged owl nods. The lark
 Rumples the blanket of the dark.

" The hoary crow pecks at his quills ;
 The fledgling tits lift up their bills.

" And in this wood, close to my door,
 I've little ones—-aye, many a score—

" Rabbits and squirrels, and young stoats—
 Whose parents died of sad sore throats.

" And young birds fallen from their nest.
 I feed them : 'tis my work loved best.

" So keep thee still ; my time's nigh gone,
 Warm thee and put more faggots on.

"The spring air's keen, and once again
  I feel the spring in my old brain.

"Thou hast blessed me: I'll bless thee back
  And stock anew thine old bare sack."

He took the sack, and where there ran
  "God loveth him that loveth man."

In lines one scarce could longer trace
  The hermit wrote with glowing face.

A minute, and the task was done.
  " Listen," said he, "then I must run : "

He loveth God who loves the toil and strife
  Of fields all soiled with sin ;
But God, He loveth the unblemished life,
  Tho' it nor toil nor spin.

He seeketh God who seeks his fellows' woes,
  And plays the martyr's part ;
But God, He seeks, wretched or happy, those
  Who would be pure in heart.

He findeth Life, who saveth his own soul,
   Crippled and scourged and crossed ;
But Life finds him, happy perhaps, and whole,
   Whoever self has lost.

Who watches alway shall at last win rest ;
   But, let them watch nor weep,
Who child-like e'er can fall upon His breast.
   Have His beloved's sleep.

The hermit rose : the man rose too,
And caught the bag the hermit threw.

With radiant face and joy-wet eyes
He stood still, speechless with surprise.

" Read it again," the hermit said,
" Ponder it o'er ; then go to bed,

" I'm off ; I've lots of things to do :
   That's my idea of Life—*for you*.

" I can't say one word more at present ;
   I've an engagement with a pheasant,

" Another time on fur and feather
  I'll chat with you for hours together.

" Goodbye—Its blithe out here and clean :
  The alleys for me are the alleys green ;

" The roof o'er me be a roof of blue
  Which the trees prop and the stars come thro'."

The hermit's voice grew faint, and died ;
The man moved—rubbed his eyes and sighed.

He found himself alone : 'Twas day,
The hut and the hermit had passed away.

On a felled tree beneath his head
Lay the last verses he had read ;

And hard by—on a leaflet torn,
Dog-eared and creased—lines nigh outworn—

There lay hid in the bracken tall
The verse he wrote upon the wall.

Smiling he put the verses by;
A skylark carolled in the sky.

A squirrel peered, frisked round and fled;
A solemn rook cawed overhead.

A moth tripped by in crimson down
Like a fine lady off to town;

And in her track, with ravenous eye,
The gauzy, gold-green dragon fly.

A rabbit munched away its care
Regardless that lean stoats were there;

And all things free, in joy's excess
Revelled in their wise carelessness—

Spoke not of pains that now were past;
Not of the troubles coming fast—

Not of things wished for—things to flee—
Spoke of the joy it is *to be.*

The man smiled, and then laughed for joy—
Laughed, and then leapt as when a boy.

The echoing wood caught up the sound ;
No more was it enchanted ground.

'Twas his—his own—aye, from his birth,
The fairest heritage of earth—

Fairer than all fair scenes afar,
Sweetest of all sweet haunts that are—

Brightest in beauty, best in tune :
England, when in her lap laughs June.

V.

OF HER HEART—THE HARVEST.

Unknown her face (serene and fair)
  The land, from end to end,
Knew her, who knew no earthly care—
  The little children's friend.

Men knew her as great souls are known,
  Afar, or haply dead,
From that outstreaming radiance thrown
  On what they've done and said.

But children—thousands knew her face,
   Careless—not more than she—
Of what the whole world called her *place*,
   Save they were round her knee.

They knew her who, when clothed and fed
   Wild to her arms they flew,
" Love Jesus, little one," she said,
   " Who more than all loves you."

They knew her—knew her radiant smile—
   Her overflowing love,
Drained of them wholly, save the while
   'Twas also stored above.

A saint ?   Aye as in cloister-cell,
   Self-scorned, self-crucified,
Dead to this world, did ever dwell
   Heaven's world-unspotted bride !

Some mental taint ?—a dream ? a craze ?
   Yea, theirs, as theirs the bliss,
Whose lives alone, unchallenged blaze
   Proofs of that world in this !

The little children's friend, child-led
   Sweet always and oft gay ;
Love Jesus, little one," she said,
   " And unto Jesus pray."

And where she prayed, no children nigh,
   None asked ; and none her bade
Tell them or where, or how, or why
   An act of Faith she made.

Unknown her past, save this one trace :
   A priest had seen her stand
Musing, a strange smile on her face,
   A strange thing in her hand.

A foreign priest of childlike mien :
   From a child's bed of pain
He'd softly passed, anon, unseen,
   To step soft back again.

He had not known, and then knew not
   The lady standing by ;
But his first word and look, I wot,
   Showed her a snow-kissed sky.

She was "The little children's friend";
   He knew that—knew her fame;
But knew not how unto the end,
   He left her a new name.

He called her—at no little loss
   To think wherefore and how—
"The lady of the broken cross
   And the Madonna's brow."

VI.

OF HIS HEART—THE RECOMPENSE.

Upon a beauteous summer's day,
   Nigh to his mansion fair:
He sat where soft winds waved the hay
   And his child's golden hair—
Toys and the journals of the day
   Lay strewn around his chair.

Of him and of his work—of all
   That he had come to be,
Those prints were full, and little gall
   In that sweet cup found he.

But now he toyed with that child's ball
    In deepest reverie.

" True "—" noble "—" lofty "—thus they ran
    The words on words he'd penned—
" In brief a good great Englishman "—
    Sated he'd reached the end.
" Now for the news ":   And he began,
    The Little Children's Friend.

The Little Children's Friend, he read ;
    And knew that morning's news
Should hush all that the *weeklies* said
    About his dreams and dues :—
The little children's Friend was dead !
    What were the last reviews ?

He'd met her not ; she *ne'er* was met
    Where speech and feast had place :
His child had met her ; and would yet
    Talk of her winning face,
And say how she should ne'er forget
    Her goodness and her grace.

"Come hither, child," and bounding gay
   She straight was on his knee :
"What said the Children's Friend that day,
   When she had romped with thee?"
"Love Jesus, and to Jesus pray ;
   But oh, how she loved *me !*

"She kissed me many times and—oh,
   Papa, she knew my name ;
And bade me love thee—love thee so,
   I ne'er could bring thee shame."
"Dear child !" he mused, " I did not know
   Such blessings sprang from fame."

VII.

OF HER HEART TO HIS—THE MESSAGE.

Gentle and large of soul and fair,
   His wife sat by his side,
And foolishly played with his hair
   As when she was his bride.

And o'er the lines that pain, thought brings,
   Her soothing hand would stray
The while she said those foolish things
   Wise women love to say :

" How is it all your thoughts are good.
  And all your writings pure ?
Scorned for so long—misunderstood,
  How did your faith endure ? "

He laughed : " What good thoughts come from
    me,
  I found them on the way.
If bright souls make bright books," said he,
  " Should mine not shine to-day ? "

" Flatterer !   But the past ?—the past ?
  Did you then know her well ? "
" Yes—for a time (it did not last)
  I lived beneath her spell."

" And wished to marry her ?—Confess ! "
  " Indeed I did, and tried ;
Till taught—how faithful none can guess—
  She was, indeed, Heaven's bride."

" *I* can: *I* ought to know her loss :
  I'm glad she kept her vow :
The lady of the broken cross
  And the Madonna's brow ! "

A kiss, a smile, and she had fled,
　Happy—thrice happy she
That he had thought the saint, now dead,
　His death to joy must be !

Softly then from its hiding-place,
　He brought forth yet again,
A little silk-lined leather case,
　And opened it—with pain ?

Aye that may be ; but with regret ?
　With pangs of foiled desire ?
Nay, but the mem'ries of a debt
　That does not irk or tire :

A few faint lines, a broken cross,
　He'd toyed with on her breast,
Epitomised the rapture, loss,
　Which they recalled—and blessed.

Years and years old were now those lines,
　Which came to him last week,
A flash of snow-capped hills and pines
　To burn, then blanch his cheek :

" From her whose prayers you did not scorn—
   Yours daily to the end.
  Love Jesus, and bid me good morn !
   The Little Children's Friend."

In Sanctuary

TRANSMITTED

" DEAR child, my mother's dead ;
But I'm *your* mother,"
This long, long since one human creature said,
And clasped another.

Then twenty-seven she
Whose child was seven ;
That child long since drew children to her knee,
Her mother in heaven.

Now by her deathbed cling
Children to mother ;
So God's love outruns time—one eddying ring
Beyond another.

184

But *our* loves eddying die,
    In rings all ravelled,
Save that, perchance, one shows us, by and by,
    Whereto they've travelled.

Iᴛ is a living thing, a tree ;
   The flowers breathe—perhaps a prayer ;
Throbbing with life, the earth—the sea !
   And why not so the air ?

The clod to roots—roots to a tree !
   All shapes from shapes less fair before :
The instinct of all things that be
   Is to be evermore.

The swallow feedeth in the air
   As stars feed swung above ;
Life has but one food everywhere,
   Which is God's love.

Moves aught so high but such might call
   Blessèd the daisied sod?
Crawls anything so mean and small
   It could creep out of God?

He loveth all in whom all thrive—
   Man, star, and breathing cell;
And whoso loveth aught alive,
   Loves he not God as well?

He loveth; and his love is taught
   Of That Love which is such,
A flower, a soul comes from Its thought,
   Vanishes at Its touch:

The hare-bell droopeth in the grass,
   The maiden fadeth on her bed;
They are infolded—do not pass,
   Nor *could* be dead.

The fair, white forehead which we know
   Shall it then be as now?
Snow melteth to become yet snow;
   Why not a brow, a brow?

Things cannot die ; they do not pass ;
   Or pass to come again :
Love biddeth things but grow—alas,
   That growth so oft is pain.

Earth soaks alike war's conduit red—
   And tears from childhood's pain !
For naught ?—when the bruised sod gives bread,
   The sifted salt-sea rain ?

The whirlwinds of forgotten prayer—
   The sigh deemed thrown away,
They live—still vibrate in the air !
   Forever useless ?—Nay !

The mad, blind soul leaps into space—
   The cankered leaf falls ere the frost ;
God sweepeth each into its place,
   How should they then be *lost ?*

Things for His care—not outwards hurled—
   Types of His love gone dim,
Parts of this seamless woven world,
   Which is a part of Him !

New Year, what hast thou that is new ?
  What themes and schemes to mark thy reign ?
What great event ; what social bent ;
  What pleasures new ; and what new pain ?

What habits to be aped or donned ;
  What shades to prove æsthetes *au fait ;*
What book, what song to catch the throng ;
  What crowning scandal of the day ?

What new idea in State or Church ?
  If *semper eadem* cries the latter,
What in the scientific search
  Of men who give their minds to matter ?

What new device for killing time ;
   And what for one another killing ;
New soap ; new socks ; new lie-packed box
   Patented to purloin a shilling ?

What knowledge new to bless the race,
   To solace suffering, stem decay ?
What new good cheer, that, year by year,
   Should gladder make each New Year's day ?

What beauty new ; new grace evolved
   From Virtue's everlasting laws ?
What purer thrills ; what nobler wills !
   What firmer bands with fairer cause ?

What sign New Year of Love's new sway ?
   What further step, what clearer view
To show, where all fade and decay,
   Lost smiles—closed eyes shall shine anew ?

TOGETHER

Love bringeth joy to Life ;
Life brings Love care.
Yet can Love only live,
As Life its best doth give :—
The Life that gives Love most has most to spare.

Life climbing seeketh Love ;
Love climbs more high ;
Life follows self-forgot ;
Love clasps it, and 'tis not :
Life lost in love is Life beyond the sky.

TO A SWEET DISSENTER

GENTLE and loveable and good,
    And with all things sincere;
What wins us most in womanhood,
    What most makes woman dear:

These things thou art; and in these things,
    Whate'er for world's unknown,
For ours there is a charm that brings
    All hearts beneath thine own.

They say thy grace is little worth:
    It is not from above;
Thine heart is set on things of earth,
    And earthly is thy love.

They say that thine immortal soul
   Is still shut up in sin :—
Thou hast ignored the Heavenly goal,
   A meaner prize to win.

They say thou needest change of heart;
   But still, it seems to me,
We'd rather have thee as thou art
   Than aught thou mightest be.

Still walk where human wants may call,
   Still work thy gracious task ;
Thy guileless life shall answer all
   That thine accusers ask.

Let others preach and teach the creeds
   Time's drifting sands record ;
Our hearts shall deeper write thy deeds,
   As done unto thy Lord.

TO AN INVALID, WITH A BUNCH OF LILIES

" CONSIDER well the lilies of the field,"
    Our blessèd Lord has taught :—
How is their glory garnered and revealed
    That toil not nor take thought !

Consider these : let their pale lips now speak
    And their pure hearts attest,
Who seeks the spears for war doth also seek
    The lilies for His breast.

Consider these : let their sweet breath now say
    How frail lives, lived unknown,
Sometimes will flood man's hot, sin-crowded way
    With incense from God's throne.

IGNORED

Hush! here's a hearse; but what of that? laugh
    on;
  Some hearse is passing somewhere every minute;
Life buds and blooms, but Death is never gone;
  Life's a gay garden with one serpent in it.

Laugh on, and have no pang when Death goes by;
  Try not to feel! Forget where grief is reigning—
Till flowers are snakes and hearts have learnt to
    die,
  And Death itself is the one flower remaining.

FROM DAY TO DAY

THEY say the leaves that left us yesterday,
   Like swallows, have but fled ;
They say the mould-clasped flowers, which were so
      gay,
   Are fast asleep—not dead.

They say each sod must change itself to roots,
   Roots to the forest glen ;
They say that brutes cease slowly to be brutes,
   Men become more than men.

They say that age but passes through decay
   Unto a fairer stage ;
They say the heart's youth cannot fade away,
   The soul has no old age.

They say that we can never lose a friend,
   And that no child can die,
That love can never come to any end
   And has no broken tie.

Because (they say) life is one flight of stairs
   To flights and flights above,
And that the bolts and bars, which we call cares,
   Are rivets of God's love.

They say, if we go up from gap to gap,
   Higher and yet more high,
This puzzling world will look like his first map
   To the explorer's eye.

They say that heaven, now always in the skies,
   Still overhead we'll see,
And that for evermore the more we rise
   The higher our heaven will be.

And still the bits that we shall see of God
   Will only be (they say)
The bits once self we on those stairs out-trod—
   Utterly wore away.

WASTE

THE countless flowers that smile and die,
   To scent their own sad tomb,
Blessing nor blessed of passer-by,
   Why should they ever bloom?

The millions of sweet-throated things
   That sing no song of glee,
Or but once spread their joyous wings,
   Why should they ever be?

The untold lone, sad hearts that wait
   Till kindred hearts may call,
And only meet when all too late,
   Why should they meet at all?

The sighs, the tears, the sweat and blood
   Of the unfruitful dead—
Strength wasted—whelmed in one waste flood,
   Why was it nursed and fed?—

Travail and death for things the use
   Whereof shall never be,
Save haply runs Waste's fetid sluice
   To some unwasting sea?

TO INQUIRE

BECAUSE I know and feel what is thy pain,
　　Thy hope and dread,
Because I know thy love—the strength, the strain,
The sweetness and the terror of the chain,
　　Which chains thee to that bed ;

Therefore in thy great love and love's great cares,
　　Where she doth languish,
My heart goes to thee, and goes with thy prayers,
Who kneelest on those bright but dreaded stairs,
　　'Twixt Heaven and anguish.

O, from that Heaven the sweetest truths be told
　　thee,
　　Anguished awhile,
Till she shall rise, or happier may behold thee,
Comfort as more than mother, smile and fold thee
　　Till thou dost smile.

DEPARTED

M. G.

FROM the fields of patient duty,
   From the paths of loving-kindness,
Through that garden-gate, whose beauty
   Blinds your eyes with sorrow's blindness.

From its purlieus whence came sleep on,
   In her fragrant soul's expansion,
To the steps, ye fall and weep on,
   Of the many-chambered mansion,

Bear her decked with flowers, as sleeping—
   Crowned with crowns our poor hands make her—
Leave her in the better keeping
   Of those hands stretched out to take her.

Saints in light, that once were mortal,
   Courage on that threshold lend her,
Onward, through each starry portal,
   Souls at home in heaven attend her.

Pardoned for all past behaviour,
   Robed in robes which angels weave her,
In the rooms prepared, her Saviour
   To His Father's house receive her.

SEMPER EADEM

ALL other things may fail or tire;
Love shall not weary nor expire.

The one thing of all things we see
That changes not, save in degree.

This man's, that child's, an angel's, thine :—
'Tis the same love—the love divine.

Beating in sunlight, bound in frost,
It is not changed, it is not lost.

There is no richer—poorer love,
One sullied here, one pure above.

The cup may dim love to our eyes;
'Tis mixed with dross, with lust, with lies;

'Tis hid; 'tis seen; 'tis choked; set free;
It is not changed, and cannot be.

It changes Time, it changes man,
Itself unchanged since Love began.

Be the sun changèd by the sod;
Yet shall not aught change Love or God.

WHAT I KNOW

I KNOW the summer's day is sweet ;
  I know that love is sweeter still ;
I know that joy is ne'er complete ;
  I know of no perpetual ill.

I know that life has many sides,
  That some things here seem hardly meet ;
I know that baseness often rides,
  While goodness walks with wearied feet.

Yet often want and wealth, I know,
  Serve each but for the other's hood ;
And spite wrongs reaped where Right did sow,
  I know hearts dance most when they're good.

I know that life, upon the whole
  Is well worth all we have to give,
And that the grander is the goal,
  So much the grander 'tis to live.

I know the grave is ever nigh,
  That evil shrinks at its faint breath ;
That only goodness makes " goodbye "
  A rainbow in the cloud of death.

SOME PEOPLE

There are some people in this world of ours,
　　　　(Who has not met them?)
Whom with her sweetest graces Nature dowers,
Or who from childhood's very earliest hours
　　　　Begin to get them.
Such are the gardeners of the heart's gay flowers,
　　　　"Tis they that set them;
"Tis they that shield them when the tempest lowers,
And when bent down and broken with the showers,
　　　　Who least forget them!
The mildest ministers that God empowers,
　　　　What powers upset them?
They walk where misery in resentment cowers;
And into hearts when other intrusion sours,
　　　　Or serves to fret them,
They pass, as Peter passed through guarded towers;
　　　　For angels let them.

ONLY ONE

THE world is full of flowers yet,
　　The heavens are bright afar ;
And life is busy, and who should fret
That earth had lost a violet,
　　Or heaven had lost a star ?

Ah ! God, if she should die—so fair—
　　Millions would smile as gay ;
But we should find no soul so rare ;
And all Thy stars would but declare
　　That ours had passed away.

THE RETURN TO SOLITUDE

UNALTERABLY beautiful and calm,
　　Thy patient, earnest eyes make fair the night,
　　Where walk thy lovers, in that tranquil light,
Drinking in strength, against the time to arm !
O solitude !　I who so knew thy charm,
　　And strayed from thee, now worsted in the fight,
　　Come to be healed and strengthened in thy might,
To walk and talk with thee till thought grows calm.
Then speak to me and teach me as of yore,
Out of the scaled mysteries of thy lore—
Teach me to smile on ills that men call fate ;
　　And, with the resolution that must win,
　　Give me that grace that marks thy lovers kin,
The patient majesty of them that wait.

15

THE PILGRIM

From a far-off golden shore,
  Stretching 'neath a tranquil sky,
From the friends that are no more,
  From the love that is gone by;
From glad days and nights as cheery
  In grand castle and calm cot,
Come I here, a pilgrim weary—
  Come from lands men say were *not*.

To a high and peaceful region,
  Light-bathed by one violet star,
Towards a red-crossed, white-plumed legion,
  Pressing up the slopes afar,
To the love that shall enfold me,
  To the glory that shall be,
Go I hence—go, men have told me,
  Seeking things I shall not see.

" Only 'twixt the shade and sheen,
　'Twixt the chasm and the sky,
'Twixt the forms that once have been
　And the faces drawing nigh,
'Twixt some old and new ideal—
　What was not, what shall not be—
E'er must live," men say, " the real
　Duped blind thing that they call *me*."

On then, on in 'circling mist ;
　Old days haunt me, new bereave me !
Be the phantoms now hope-kissed,
　Memory's ghosts that shall deceive me !
Let ideals e'er enfold me,
　(And illusions when they must)
So know I earth cannot mould me,
　Who but for this hour am *dust !*

In Tenebris

I.

SUMMER and Winter, seed and harvest time,
  The bright, long days, brief dark ones—as of
      yore ;
Spring flowers, and forests, waving in their prime—
  In each place always what has been before ;
And everywhere always, in every clime,
  The heart that yearns for what will be no more !

Smiles waking smiles ; and sighs invoking sighs,
  Wander where'er we may, hide where we will.
In each place, always 'neath the eternal skies,
  The world's eternal heart-throb, pang and thrill ;
And nowhere ever but eyes fixed on eyes,
  Lips pressed to lips forever closed and still.

A platitude? An obvious fact? Not so—
  Not when the Spring flowers follow Winter's rain,
Hearts leap to hearts, sad sundered long ago—
  When eyes meet eyes, lips cling to lips again;
And, plunged beneath Life's joy-flashed waves we
    know
How dark, how still Death's plumbless sea of
    pain!

II.

" Hail, poor wretch! Once more thee only,
  This time, welcomely I meet,
Shivering, shelterless, and lonely,
  In the rain-swept, empty street.

" Fashionless thy coat and faded,
  'Tis the same I note, as when,
Fluff-strewn, through gay throngs it waded,
  Sporting flowers one gave thee then.

"Old and haggard—tho' thou pilest
  Paint and rouge on thy cracked face!
Vain, to hide thy plight thou smilest,
  Vain wouldst speed thy shambling pace.

" Come with me to feed and sup,
    Slouch and mumble I advise thee ;
All thy calm, grand ' making up '
    Can but torture—not disguise thee :

" We have met too oft.   Too rarely
    Have we supped and talked at ease.
Do those tottering limbs oft barely
    Keep thee upright ?   So do these !

" Are those watery, red-veined eyes
    Able scarce thy path to see ?
Come !—To thee I'll tell no lies—
    Soon it will be so with me.

" Are there homes and hearts that need thee,
    That my door thou shouldst go by ?
Wouldst thou rave with one who'll heed thee ?
    Come ; in such a case am I."

Half in pity, half derision,
    Thus, hale and in manhood's pride,
Spake a strong man to the vision
    Of a weak one by his side.

Spake as unto one he saw,
    One from whom no incitation
Either jape or jest could draw,
    In his calm, dumb tribulation.

And that mocked, mute ghost, I ween,
    Of a tottering man, strength-shorn,
Was the strong man's shadow, seen
    In the fierce light of his scorn.

" Vain the storm wails now, and vainer
    Want and pain go howling by ;
Safe, old starched and rouged campaigner,
    With barred doors speak you and I.

" Off thy pads and paint and plaster !
    Ruthless, rip thy cloak apart :
Show me naked thy disaster—
    Show me thy lean, wrinkled heart.

" Ah, I knew.   Thy brave disguise
    Ill concealed what now I see—
What ?   The picture all men's eyes
    Soon, soon will behold in *me* ?—

" But a baser kind of cheating
    Makes me now seem young and brave ?
Sound *my* heart, and note its beating,
    Rhythmic as the ocean wave !

" Smilest thou, and not in scorn ?
    Yes, I sometimes feel as thou ;
Nathless where the masks *I've* worn ?—
    Let the mob's eyes rake me now.

" Let them search, probe !—Heaven preserve me
    From such quakes !—what didst thou see ?
Ghosts ?   Let aught shock me, unnerve me,
    Find me out as I found thee !

" Poor, scared wreck, why look behind thee ?
    Sooth, thy heart then nearly stopped !
Shrivelled ?— dwarfed ?— One scarce can find
      thee,
    Now thy brave attire is dropped.

" Smilest thou again ?—in pity ?
    God, that thou shouldst pity *me !*
Talk we then, as in this city
    No boon souls could talk as we.

"Tell me what those eyes saw round thee—
　　What they thought or longed to see,
　When I, lonely, shivering, found thee ;
　　Save (Heaven knows) thou foundest me.

" Friends of old, forgot, forsaken ?
　　Nay, that cant becomes thee not ;
　Rooks from nests on trees storm-shaken !
　　Rats that smelt the hulk's dry rot !

"Thy fault ?　They were true and kind ?
　　Say so if it pleases thee ;
　Boots it now what puff of wind
　　Started ships across the sea ?

" Friends now thine—the few, that still
　　Powerless love and fear to pain thee ?
　Ah, what their restraint or will
　　To the power that *did* sustain thee ?

" Friendship is a plant that shoots
　　Fast enough, and flowers free :
　See it smiling round the roots
　　Of that great, green fallen tree !

" He thy friend was—he thy shelter !
   Slighted, looked he powerless on,
When suns smote, and helter-skelter
   Storms came and the flowers were gone ?

" Lovers then ?   Did their eyes glimmer,
   Star-like from the mist again,
As the smoke-choked sky drew dimmer
   Through the bleak, wind-rifted rain ?

" Come, of lovers thou hadst plenty :
   Did they all prove false or frail ?
Oh, Love's cup, when thou wast twenty !
   Cup ?   Thou drankest from a pail !

" Sum them up : 'Twould turn thee dizzy—
   Eyes made love to, eyes love made !
Idler ! but thou once wast busy :
   In thy youth Love was thy trade.

" Smilest ?—and not in derision ?
   Ah, of course, thy wandering ken
Ever sought that rapturous vision,
   Goddess-rained on sons of men.

" Well, it came, or something near it—
    What, thy thunder-blackened brow,
  Browbeats me ?   I do not fear it ;
    But, poor wretch, what fearest thou ?

" Nay, 'tis now my turn to pity :
    Hug that memory—put it by ;
  Who should spare thee in this city ?
    Who should pity if not I ?

" Faith, now I could half revere thee,
    Who should call thee base and mean—
  Canting, say I loathe and fear thee :
    Heavens ! to think what thou hadst been !—

" Hadst been—shouldst have been—nigh wast !
    Clench those trembling, twitching hands :
  Would they clutch Life's robe long lost ?
    Catch Time's long strained golden sands ?

" No ? Then from Love's first-scorned gladness—
    Withered smiles and parched, pale eyes ;
  From its last-gulfed starry madness,
    Come to days when thou wast wise—

" When so wise, so strong and calm,
　　Saidst thy heart, ' But give me rest,
　Circled of that gentle arm,
　　On that kind, pure, faithful breast.'

" Well, and what proved thy desire?
　　What thy wise heart's latest quest?
　What those charms to goad nor tire?
　　Did there yet remain a rest?

" Who the deeper dreams, and later,
　　Blinks more at the blaze of day !
　And are pangs for angels greater
　　When they've flown ; or turned to clay?

" Sated of the flowers moth-sipped,
　　Adder-stung of the gods' wine,
　' Bread !' thou criedst, hunger-whipped :
　　Was it given ?　Wouldst it were thine?

" Given, had it not proved a stone ?—
　　Bridling?　Burns thy cracked cheek ?　What,
　Must I leave *that* love alone?
　　Then to Hades with the lot !

" Not the warmth and not the splendour
    Of thy soul's divinest days ;
Not her nights most starry-tender
    Found she in Love's fairest ways.

" For those fires the fiercest yearning
    Brought but woman's hands the coal—
Sputtering fires, now scarcely burning
    In thy white-ashed dismal soul ?

" Rake them up ! Remember ! Dream !
    Not again ? Well, weep not booby :
Once o'er Life's dull mud-banked stream
    Shot their shafts of gold and ruby !

" Once ? Eh, what ? Those wandering glances
    Say some gleam has not yet fled—
O'er thy palsied old heart dances ?
    Flits thro' thy dim cobwebbed head ?

" Come then, laugh to see men store
    Sodom's apples ! Thine were sweet !
Wanderer from Time's gem-strewn shore,
    Chaff those hucksters in the street.

"Cry, ' In vain they grub and grumble ;
　　Thy toil,' say, ' was sweet as wine '—
　' Dust their works to dust will tumble !'
　　Show them some grand bit of thine.

" Give it to them—if they'll take it ;
　　Scorned, were it then less a gem ?
　Rakers of the garbage rake it
　　For choice garbage : what of *them* ?

" *Thy* works were to please the wise, .
　　Very few in all the ages ;
　Had they charmed the ' Beast's seven eyes ?'
　　Say they had been bestial pages.

" Do the gods in pledge not keep
　　All scorned things they've stamped divine,
　Hiding them while counted cheap ?
　　Lord !   What thou hast pawned of thine !

"' Think of that ; then laugh, and jingle
　　All thy current sovereigns left,
　While, to grab Life's counters, mingle
　　Black-nailed greed and white-gloved theft.

" Eye the magnates of each town,
    Smiling from calm heights sublime,
How on dust-heaps of Renown,
    Squat the rag-pickers of Time !

" Heaven forgive me : thou *dost* smile—
    Fairer smile has ne'er adorned thee ;
Is it then, now, not worth while
    To reflect the stars have scorned thee ?

" Speak ! Rebuke me, stone-like sad,
    Staring at that face above thee,
And shall I, whom it turns mad,
    For thy better soul not love thee ?—

" Love thee, whom I now should hate,
    Or thou me—whom, hand in glove,
Long he loved, he whom too late,
    O God, how we both do love !

" Gone, who gave those dreams their bloom ;
    Hope its breath ; lost hours their sigh !
Does *thy* voice now break the gloom ?
    Which art thou ; and which am I ?

" Shall I find myself again,
    Sport of tears and scorn pain-fed :
No illusive ray ; but vain,
    Long vain dreams of him that's dead ! "

And the silence reigned again,
    Save that in the deepened gloom,
Sobbed the storm against the pane,
    'Twixt the sobbings in the room,

Till a meek, low voice inquired,
    " Which the sweetest hour appears—
Most to be again desired—
    Which the best of manhood's years ? "

Long the pause and low the sigh,
    Not of pain, not of desire :—
" Nay I cannot tell, not I ;
    Which sparks least turn tow to fire ?

" What fire burns with the least pain ?
    What pain soonest leaves one gay ?
What glad thing proves least in vain ?
    What vain breath blows last away ?

" Haply—how I cannot tell—
 'Twas some hour, of toil left sweet,
When, from some dim tower, the bell
 Bade me look o'er woods and wheat.

"Oft with him—how I remember—
 Life *was* sweet ; nor sweet in vain
Came the colours of September,
 Came the scents in April rain.

"Oft with him and her beside me,
 Hopes—how fair—at morn took root—
Bloomed, storm-swayed, nor yet denied me,
 When Eve came, uncankered fruit.

" But to find the sweetest, best
 Of those hours thus best beguiled,
When brief toil won some brief rest,
 Where brief joy unconscious smiled --

" Oh, I can't : As bees to heather,
 Bloom to Summer, rills from rain,
Came they, varied as the weather—
 Came ; and come back now with pain !

" Oh, the times ; and oh, the places,
  When — where — (children — flowers know
    how) —
Those two voices those two faces,
  Made life sweet as bitter now.

" Yea, the children, and the flowers,
  And the one who may not speak ;
They know how to crowd the hours
  With the joy whose shreds we seek.

" For as all bliss flies below
  Tell me of none grasped above,
Save of lilies as they grow,
  Save of children as they love."

And the silence reigned again,
  Save for foot-falls on the floor,
And the gusts against the pane,
  And the creaking of a door.

Then out of the gloom apace
  Stepped a woman into sight ;
And the man smiled in her face,
  And the room was filled with light.

Where ?   Wherever, haply late,
   Seas suck back some flakes of foam,
Wherein some man laid the great
   Pillars of his heart and home.

When ?   Each day, when by some sod,
   O'er some wild heart's storm, He saith,
" Be still : know that I am God,
   Who the seas hold, and thy breath——"

Where from heaps of Life's carved stones,
   Ornaments and crevice-grass,
Some voice in the *débris* groans
   Vanitatum vanitas !—

Where some soul that anguish wrings,
   And the flesh no more can cow,
Beats its strong indignant wings,
   Asking, "Can'st thou find me *now ?* '

III.

As leaves whirled down the withered glade,
　　Stars from the blackened sky ;
As flowers where rain and sunshine played,
Gone from the clean-swept path, white made,
　　Where blizzards hurtled by :—
Hope's fairy-peopled shining strand,
And Memory's sweet-ghost-haunted, and old-song-
　　echoing land !
Gone as the shadow with the shape,
As broideries with the breast they drape,
As warmth with the fire !　What light is not wan,
When the light of our eyes lay in eyes that are
　　gone ?

IV.

Because that he had lived nigh four score years,
　　And knew no breaking up—
Because Life's only dregs, which were our tears,
　　He drank out of Death's cup—

Because his eye was dimmed not, and Life's race
　　Enthralled him to the last—
Because he died asleep, and his loved face
　　Looked loveliest as life passed—

Because in Life we talked and planned always,
    And in Death could but chat ;
And not once said he, thinking of these days,
    " Do this " or " Don't do that "—

Because he owned he had been satisfied
    With boons more than desired ;
And (the first time in life, the hour he died)
    He said to us, " I'm tired ! "—

Because thus meetly, still Life's warm red ray
    Shone where we lost his track,
And soon he'd gone at dark, and thro' decay,
    Can we less wish him back ?

For all that wisdom teaches—understands,
    Can we less long, to-day,
To find and press those kind and busy hands,
    Clasped in that bed of clay ?

They tell us kindly that he has not died ;
    His soul but hence has sped.
Ah, no : his soul, voice, glance all here abide,
    And all say, " He is dead."

His foot rings on the step ; he stands and calls
　　Our names by every door ;
Passing, he straightens pictures on the walls,
　　Picks books up from the floor.

He prunes the rose trees that he loves ; and throws
　　The wild birds still their seed ;
From pane to pane, thro' the wet day he goes ;
　　Sits statue-like to read.

His soul remains with us ; and every day
　　Something we've seen or read,
We think (and almost to each other *say*)
　　" We must tell "—him who's dead.

Dead ! Let them juggle with that word who yet
　　Taught not its meaning dare :—
To hear and turn to see, and not forget
　　He can no more be there !

" No more—no more ! "　That cry goes on, until
　　We hold our trembling breath,
Listen, and think we hear that voice grown still,
　　" There shall be no more Death."

No more vain hopes? regrets? Care's tangled skein
   For dreams of woven bliss?
Yea all, if that which was may be again ;
   And never, never this !

Speak !—Say, dear voice (how would we now be
    said ?)
   " There is a golden shore "—
(How would we seek it, now that thou art dead ?)
   " Where Death shall be no more."

Speak to us of Life's never-drooping tree,
   Whereof the leaves heal pains,
Who wounded 'neath the willows speak of thee,
   And of the bloom Death stains—

Who think of thee whene'er we kneel to pray ;
   Nor less of God, but rather
More earnestly—more pondering what we say,
   Whene'er we say " Our Father."

Speak to us when we dream—long dreams and
    say,
   As to and fro they dart,
These formless shapes are shadows, in *some* ray.
   From substance where thou art.

Speak to us of the morning and the waking—
    Of the unwavering light,
Who from Faith's watch-tower, with dim eyes and
      aching,
    Call after thee " Good-night."

Speak to us as to children, so that we,
    Childlike in heart and mind,
Thy great, kind, constant love can never see,
    And doubt God loves mankind.

Speak, who so soon of all our faults made light—
    So bade our last fret cease,
Of that Forgiveness which is infinite,
    And of His Perfect Peace.

Helene

A LITTLE tale complete in little parts,
Gleaned from his garret's litter, and his heart's—

A dreamer's tale, who to himself would tell
The things he dreamed and think that they befell.

Thus would he make himself, nor deem it vain,
Some sweet abode on some large fair domain.

Mirth, pleasure, even happiness, alas !
Made he of dreams, then dreamt they would not
    pass ;

Until, at last, so very apt grew he
To make and love the things he wished to be,

He made, nor dreamt he'd made, for some long
    while—
Let the wise ponder and the foolish smile—

A beauteous damsel, whom thus made full-grown
He looked on, loved, and straightway called his
    own.

And this the tale of that sweet maid he told,
As he beheld her or could not behold,

Gleaned from the litter that he left behind,
The litter of his garret, and his mind.

Haply 'twill serve to fill some dreamer's head,
Turning some dreamless moments on his bed.

Haply some wise soul wide awake may smile,
And sleep from wisdom for a little while.

There's little chance that he will smile or weep,
Let the wise nod, or fools stir in their sleep.

He might have died—that is, have passed away
To the long dreamless night, some wise folk say ;

Some, counted fools, say to the morning light
Whose bloom of dreams no waking shrouds nor
    night.

Perchance he's gone abroad or sails the sea ;
He may, God wot, be hiding near to me.

I only know that he went out one day
And came not back, and never will folk say :

He fled, grief-maddened by some shaft of doom ;
His friend, I took to his disordered room—

Paid little bills and burnt—a task more bitter—
Reams of his writings, bundles of his litter,

Among the which I found and set apart
These chapters of a tale told to his heart—

A tame but a complete one as I learnt,
Keeping each portion marked "not to be burnt."

At first, my wayward conscience thus to cheat,
I thought I'd throw them out into the street.

And then I mused for all that now is said,
He may not have gone mad, nor yet be dead.

In years to come he might come back and say,
" Why did you throw my little dream away ?—

" My little chain of dreams, whereof each link
Was something that the thoughtful cannot think.—

Whereof the whole, let mind inquire of mind,
Hid something that the wise ones cannot find ? "

Thus dreamers talk—thus ever taunt the schools
With skill to teach all save what makes men fools.

Thus bared he oft his pride and gloated on't,
Wanting few ills but consciousness of want.

And when want found him—haply hunger's pains,
He was but as a traveller changing trains.—

A moment on the platform : wet or fine,
What mattered it ? he soon was on the line,

Seeing through the dyed windows of his brain,
What others see through *Bradshaw* and the pane.

My friend! So for old friendship's smiles and
    tears,
And for that half-feared ghost, of coming years,

I print his little love-dream as I found it,
With his room's litter and his life's around it.

And if perchance it proves a charm to steal
Into one heart, and make that one heart feel

Sweetness or motion—some new sense of powers,
Such as rains give to rills, the dew to flowers,

It would have pleased him ; for 'twas that he said—
That sense assuring souls they are not dead,

The which who find find knowledge—haply woe,
And wisdom's ways of pleasure, who bestow.

I.

After the sunshine sweetness
    In sod and flower and tree ;
After the floods the fleetness
    Of streamlets to the sea

From summer winds sweet motion
  In all that floats and flies;
From climbed snow-peaks a notion
  Of God's pure changeless skies.

And thoughts like flowers for whiteness;
  Dreams of what earth might be,
From her who brought the brightness,
  And breath of heaven to me.

II.

Bring me loads of lilies,
  Pure and spotless fair,
To deck her charms,
And fill her arms
  And shower upon her hair:
Lilies of the vale,
Graceful, gentle pale,
  For her the graceful, gentle one, and
    fairest of the fair.

Bring me heaps of violets,
  Dewy-eyed and sweet,
Her charms to deck
And wreathe her neck,

And scatter round her feet :
Violets of the wood,
Self-forgotten, good,
   For her the self-forgotten one, and
      sweetest of the sweet.

Bring me lilies, violets,
   Her flowers, to be caressed—
Her lips to taste,
And clasp her waist,
   And peep into her breast :
None but fresh and sweet ones,
All spotless-hearted, meet ones
   For her to me the fairest one, the
      sweetest and the best.

III.

You say my verses were not true ;
   Then tell me how you know :—
Should violets tell who love their smell—
   Lilies their hearts of snow ?

And must she say, who acts, as they,
   Life's true unconscious part,
How much she flung joy in my way,
   And goodness in my heart ?

Oh yes, of you my verse was true ;
   But is it—should it be,
You have one thought with sorrow fraught
   That it was true of me ?

Ah, no.   I'll give that fear no room,
   Where Hopes so thickly throng—
One speck on mem'ry's mass of bloom,
   One false note in her song !

Must joy bring care, be mine that share ;
   Should flower or star that shone,
Regret its light and sweetness, where
   One sighs that it is gone ?

It was—*is* true, whate'er betide—
   Song made nor stayed, so true,
It *comes* and put me on one side,
   As God's smile so treats you.

IV.

ST. VALENTINE'S EVE.

Hail to the Patron Saint of mine
   And every love-plagued heart,
Who now—where men flout not his shrine
   Steps in to play his part.

Through many a pane he peers to-night—
   (Blessings upon his track !)
And says : "Your Valentine now write ;
   And pitch it in my sack."

And so in haste I write to you,
   Whom you have often met ;
But whom, my dear, you never *knew*,
   And so will not forget.

Shall *I* forget or how or when
   Our days and ways were twined—
The sketches of you I made then
   All o'er my heart and mind?

17

But now—and this is why I write—
    They say " my eyes weren't true :—
I've got you all in a wrong light—
    Those pictures aren't like you."

They say—but surely they are blind—
    " You weren't like that and this :
Nor thus and thus":—They scarce can find
    One feature not amiss.

Tho' they don't *say* you had brown eyes
    And locks of jet-black hair,
They'd almost have me ask (with sighs)
    If you were *really fair !*

Who "they" may be and where they dwell,
    Perchance you know ; not I :—
" They " are those little birds that tell
    Things in the ear, and fly.

" You leaned *that* way, not this ; your pose
    Is my artistic stuff—
Your eyes are turned too low ; your nose
    Is not turned up enough ! "

Mine was, my dear, when they said that :
    I wondered how " they " drew ;
And what the mischief they'd be at,
    If they for me sketched you.

They could but make you fair, I know ;
    They'd give you height, my dear ;
They'd think they'd make you grand ; but oh,
    You *would* look cramped and queer—

I mean those little flying birds,
    Whose bodies melt, I wis ;
Whose souls drop—little dying words—
    Dead, on the face I kiss.

The face I've framed and shield from harm,
    And wear Heaven's aid to win—
The sort of little holy charm
    That keeps a man from sin.

And if no more I see that face,
    Naught soon shall make me see
A dwarfed, dimmed likeness in its place,
    To steal my charm from me.

Goodness !　He's rapping at my pane,
　St. Valentine, dear saint !
So if I ne'er write you again,
　Goodbye ; and you I'll paint.

I've sketches of you good enough
　To last me all my days,
Models, ideals, and artists " stuff "
　To win the wide world's praise—

Not yours : I'd burn them—at the stake,
　Rather than think to see
You turn to things that I might make
　From things that might make me—

Such things as made me, such as made
　The world I lived in too,
My powers, my views, my stock-in-trade
　When I was *drawing* you.

I *drew* you—close ; and you were glad ;
　If now the things I paint
Perchance must often make me sad—
　He's off (One word—*dear* Saint !)

That was for him ; 'twould do for you
And now if till we die ;
Or if till (Here I'll pitch it through)
Alas, *ma belle !*—Goodbye !

V.

You come in the still night, Helene,
Less often in the day,
Sometimes a smile of light, Helene,
That smiles and flits away ;
But oftest sad and white, Helene,
Without a word to say.

And I look back at you, Helene,
With smiles when you are gay ;
But oftest blankly too, Helene,
As looks a face of clay :—
There's nothing I can do, Helene,
I know not what to say.

Save thus I ne'er may look, Helene,
On you or you on me :—

We sat and read one book, Helene—
　It seemed of things to be :
We liked it : Then one took, Helene,
　Nay, snatched it off your knee.

They may have shown you what, Helene,
　To me has not been shown ;
Perhaps they chose your lot, Helene ;
　Perchance you chose your own,
You may ; and you may not, Helene,
　Sometimes that lot bemoan.

Thus oft in the still night, Helene,
　Less often in the day,
You look all sad and white, Helene,
　Upon my face as clay ;
But may be gay and bright, Helene,
　And may think I am gay.

I might learn what is true, Helene—
　If cared for or forgot,—
What's like to spread things through, Helene,
　The brightness or the blot ;
But save I learn from you, Helene,
　You only, I shall not.

Till then or till we're dead, Helene,
  I'll keep, as framed to-day,
That sad white face instead, Helene,
  To which I've naught to say,
Torn from the book we read, Helene,
  When it was snatched away.

VI.

And wouldst thou that we said goodbye?
  Why then, goodbye it must be.
And wouldst thou that my hopes should die?
Why then, they're dead : I can but sigh,
  Bereavèd, " Dust to dust be."

" In sure and certain hope——? " ah, no :
  That is for Death's dark portal—
That is the heart-wrung cry of woe
For something lost, but which we know
  Was something born immortal.

Love comes immortal as the soul,
  And goes, alas, when driven :
We lose love ; but none ever stole,
Begged it or won in any *rôle*—
  Immortal things are given.

Given were thy charms of soul and face ;
  Given my poor love alack—
Such things are thine of right, not grace,
Gifts that wear out, but in no case
  Were ever taken back.

If true then is it sad that I
  To love unloved am fated ?
But not for me that bitter cry
Of hearts wrung o'er those graves where lie
  The loves their loves created.

Sad must I see the wealth, the charms
  Of Love I wished were mine ;
Unloved, whence were Love's throbs—alarms ?
But oh, the anguish of those arms
  Which held and then lost thine !

So if thy *heart* would say goodbye,
  Why then goodbye it must be :
The dream was sweet, and sadly I
Stoop o'er that sweet, pure face and sigh,
  Kissing it, " Dust to dust be."

And I would wish thee Love to know;
 And never, at Death's portal,
That all too common pang of woe
For Love *lost* ere its age and snow
 Announce its youth immortal.

ADDENDUM

I.

I ask thee not what seekest thou,
 Nor wherefore dost thou come,
Dumb ghost, where all is ghostly now,
 And all the ghosts are dumb.

Pallid the sun-glints, glum the showers,
 Ghostly the swallow's wing,
The hawthorn and the lilac flowers
 But joyless wraiths of spring!

Silence what had been song and glee,
 Shadow all he'd made shine;
And, where a thousand ghosts make free,
 Why should I question thine?

Save only that, in duskier nooks,
   It stands or moves apart,
And meets me timidly, and looks
   Deeper into my heart—

Looks and flits past with pallid cheek,
   And with a questioning eye,
Too frail to let that wronged heart speak,
   Too pure to make a lie.

Then must I think, in deepened gloom,
   With half-remorseful woe,
How in that hushed, white-flower-filled room—
   O God, how long ago !—

In the last hour when I could gaze
   On all there was to see
Of him whose love and pride and praise
   Was Life's strong wine to me,

To those last tokens love had brought,
   Many and sweet and rare,
I turned from his white face, and sought
   The one that was not there.

II.

Red is the rowan tree,
　The swifts begin to fly,
The ling brings back the bee ;
And where thou broughtest me
　Again come I.

Full is each purple bell
　Of honey for the bee ;
But why, I cannot tell
Are the beauty and the spell
　Of the bare crag for me.

Gone that fair dream so fleet,
　Gone the keen after-pain ;
Ice vanished in the heat,
Scorn bitter in tears sweet :—
　Why dost thou still remain ?

Welcome red Autumn's charms,
　Come Winter's threatening sky—
Bring to me hopes, alarms,
Life's hurricanes and calms ;
　But thou, go by.

By the belovèd dead
　With requiems laid I thee ;
Why on that rose-heaped bed
Rest not thy gentle head,
　And let me be ?

What matter if the loss
　Was mine or thine or ours ;
Must rains not green the moss
Because tears shine, as dross,
　On withered flowers ?

Sweetly the dead sleeps now ;
　Then, where pale heath bells blow,
Pure as thy pure sweet brow,
Sleep here, beloved, sleep thou,
　And let me go.

Erin Mavourneen

THE CAR OF FORTUNE

IF Fortune said just now to me,
  " Wish, quick : your heart I'll gladden,"
I'd say, " Then bring a car, machree,
  And drive to Ballyshadden.

" And call in London as we go
    For Kathleen—say O'Grady ;
  Then whip round, by the *Pays de Vaud*,
    For the old hall's gracious lady.

" And back to Erin call my boy—
    Aye call : he'll come for me,
  Whose fresh young heart brought mine the joy
    Of rain to a raft at sea.

" And bid him bring that winsome child
  To sing for me the *Shan Van Voch*,
 Whose dream-fair eyes shone as calm skies
  Mirrored on dim deep Glendeloch.

" And all the clan of sport and fun—
  Those men and maids arraign,
 (Friends of the saddle, line, and gun)
  Halloo them back again.

" Then let us to the Fox's Glen,
  That gorse-hemmed gold and green morass,
 Like Erin's flag flung o'er the men
  Whose pikes there dyed the grass.

" There we will track the water-fowl ;
  Anon fish fair Loch Dan :
 And climb the frock of the White Nun Rock
  For the woodquests of Dun Rhan.

" Again we'll shoot and ride all day
  On mountain, moor, and sand ;
 And sail at eve on the sun-shot bay
  That flows by the silver strand.

"'Then under the stars, in saddles and cars,
    Sated of things that gladden,
  Back to that haunt of peace we'll jaunt,
    In the Vale of Ballyshadden.

"'Then supper and, ho ! by the log-fire glow,
    Sleep wooed with the jest and the riddle !
  Or sleep may go hang, let one mischievous twang
    Suggest that we dance to the fiddle !

"And the last thing the best: when apart from
    the rest,
    For Kathleen's good-night I have tarried,
  I will just—for why not ? Wisha ! then, I forgot ;
    For Kathleen's in London and married !

"And what ?—How is this ? Where's the car
    What's amiss ?
    Ho, Wicklow's blue hills and bright beaches,
  The divil a jot is there left of the lot
    But a brogue and a pair of knee-breeches !

THE sun falls with a filmy glow
   On fields of English corn,
And well in English woods I know
   His smile at eve and morn.

And on the sleep-steeped face of France
   He tints the verdant vine;
And the Juras, 'neath his splintered lance,
   Gush as with purple wine.

And oft on many an Alpine spire
   I've watched the sunset throw
A carmine mantle fringed with fire
   Upon the cold white snow.

But of all light or far or nigh
   I've ever loved to see,
The light I loved in Ireland's Eye
   Comes oftest back to me—

An isle of shadow and of sheen
   Clasped with a belt of spray,
Where purple-black folds golden-green,
   Like night at sport with day—

Where white wings flash in violet mist,
   Bright sails through shadows glide,
Where pearl goes pink, when crags are kissed
   By the calm sunset tide

In summer and winter, storms and calms,
   When children crossed to play,
When dead brave men slept in your arms,
   Their boats wrecked in the bay,

I've looked with them who look no more:
   Isle of my brightest dreams,
Apart, we've sailed from your still shore,
   Out of your golden beams.

The morn will smile on that sweet isle ;
   And oft at sunset hour
There'll be figures seen on its summit green,
   And its grey Martello tower ;

But not, not ours, who meet no more—
   Who loved and said goodbye,
To love when has vanished Erin's shore
   And the light in Ireland's Eye.

THE ONE I LOVE

WE rove the cliffs beside the sea,
    And watch the ships go by,
And make our plans for years to be,
    The one I love and I.

And oft we creep out on the rocks,
    Far from the golden shore,
And start the gulls in screaming flocks,
    When the white breakers roar.

Anon we fly before the storm,
    And laugh to be so free ;
The sea-caves keep us snug and warm,
    The one I love and me.

And every pool-ringed rock we know,
　　And every inch of sand,
And where the secret currents flow,
　　And where a boat can land.

The fisher-folk they know us well,
　　The one I love and me ;
And much they muse, and talk, and tell
　　About the things they see.

They say we go like lines of foam,
　　All whirling wild and gay,
Not like those fin-locked things that roam
　　In couples by the bay.

Yes, oft we swoop and circle glad
　　As the gay gulls above ;
But sometimes we are very sad—
　　I and the one I love—

So sad, we sigh and mutely creep
　　Into some gorsy cleft,
And watch the far white waves that leap
　　To the sea-weed they have left.

And then the wide, wet, empty strand
   Can almost make us cry ;
We know, and take each other's hand,
   The one I love and I.

I see no more the white-specked boat
   Float on the far blue rim ;
For sudden mists which round me float
   Have made my eyes grow dim.

But no, we do not hug our pain,
   That soon we'll say goodbye ;
For well we know we'll meet again,
   The one I love and I.

And so we scramble down the cliff
   And make each other gay ;
And chase away that hovering " if,"
   As swifts that chase a jay.

The gorse will keep its golden bloom,
   The gulls will sail above ;
And we'll be true while skies are blue,
   I and the one I love.

And men and things and years may pass,
　　As ships that pass the bay ;
And Time, it will bring change, alas !
　　But we'll keep faith alway.

The one I love will never change
　　So that our love mayn't be ;
Nor maid nor manhood shall estrange
　　That bright, bold boy and me.

BY LOUGHNALOO

Say not that we may meet no more,
  Who met at Loughnaloo;
My heart drifts oft to that still shore
  Where drifted I to you.

Of Erin's gifts the best, you came
  That quiet hour to me,
When sundown set the gorse aflame
  That fringed the bright, blue sea,

My heart had wandered far away
  Across that strip of blue;
But came back, with the doves that day,
  To sleep at Loughnaloo.

For we had met; and oh, how oft
 Met we in those spring days,
Ere the primrose sank in the sedgy croft,
 And the king-cup caught ablaze.

Daily we saw the filmy cloud
 Of bluebells fill the glade ;
And the hawthorn's fairy-blossom crowd
 Form, and flutter, and fade.

We plucked the great gold-flagon flowers
 By many a stream and swamp ;
And still we met in the merry hours
 When the poppies came out to romp.

And when the heather met the gorse,
 Still met and dallied we,
As the sedge-grass with the water-course,
 And the seaweed with the sea.

In all my moods, or light, or grave,
 Your influence had its part,
The sweetest friend God ever gave
 Unto a lonely heart.

And then we parted—with a sigh—
   The flowers had run their course ;
But of no dead bloom breathed our " goodbye "
   In the ever-golden gorse.

And some sweet day adrift once more
   As sweet shall I find you,
Be it but on that farther, more golden shore
   Than the shore of Loughnaloo !

COLLEEN MACHREE

Oh, *la belle France*
 Is *spirituelle:*
I've known the glance
 Of her *demoiselle*
Make dead hearts dance
 To their passing-bell.

The donna of Spain
 I've seen, *sans peur,*
Without thought of stain,
 Kill of *hommes de cœur*
More than ever were slain
 By a *beau sabreur.*

266

And in Milan
   I've known, I've seen a
Sibyl-taught Pan—
   Swayed Signorina
Play with poor man
   À la concertina.

But from Seville,
   Milan, *Paris,*
With added zeal,
   Colleen Machree,
Once more I kneel
   Enslaved to thee.

Musha, my dear,
   Your eyes are true ;
Nor flash ; nor fear
   Who looks them through,
A sea of clear,
   Deep, sunlit blue !

Those southern eyes,
   For me they glow

As burning skies
  On mountain snow,
In whose warmth sighs
  The vale below.

Cold on his breast
  Their beams are thrown,
Whose memories blest
  Dwell in those lone,
Cool haunts of rest,
  Where smile thine own.

Oh, bright, kind, wise
  Colleen Machree,
Oh, land whose skies
  Through tears I see,
Thine are the eyes,
  The haunts for me !

Then fade Seville,
  Milan, *Paris :*
The heart they'd steal,
  To spurn may be,
Sore, thou didst heal,
  Colleen Machree !

Say shall we meet in London town ;
    Or in *le beau Paris ;*
Or where the slumberous sun sinks down
    On *bella Napoli ?*

And shall we quaff the nut-brown ale
    To lend our hearts a glow, boy ;
Or drain a cup, to rouge them up,
    Of red wine from Bordeaux, boy ?

And shall we smoke the Broseley pipe,
    Swiss, German, Dutch and divers ;
Weeds bagged *en tour*, a *Londres, Cavour*,
    Your sweet and strong *straight fivers ?*

Not there we'll meet—not thus we'll greet ;
　　But as in days afar, dear,—
Where every ache got an Irish wake—
　　When Time was a jaunting-car, dear !

There, thus we'll smoke the old *dudheen*
　　(St. Cevan and O'Toole)
And toast, unchallenged, in potheen
　　Our "ginuine Home-Rule."

We'll jaunt around the days gone by,
　　And knock old memories up ;
And with the sad ghosts we will sigh,
　　And with the gay we'll sup.

We'll hold the wake of dear Old Sake—
　　Hopes, dreams, ambitions fled, dear ;
We'll prop them up with pipe and cup,
　　Till one can't tell they're dead, dear.

Joy's olden golden threads we'll weave
　　Till Life's one glorious maze
Of Easter and All Hallow Eve
　　Starred with St. Patrick's Days.

But when? say when—Och! could my pen
  But speed that blessèd day, dear,
Fast Time should glide, till Life's dull tide
  Flashed into Dublin Bay, dear!

THE SILENCE OF BALLYRAGHAN

The long, red drive was a miry dun,
    The step moss-green ; and on the door
Lay thick, black webs, all long since spun,
And snail paths, burnt in by the sun,
    And stains from the wet and the winter's hoar.

The woodquests cooed in the lime tree there,
    The jackdaws chattered in the sky ;
I heard the brook, where the stones were bare,
And the moor-hens in their sedgy lair,
    As in the sweet old days gone by.

From the garden-gate two rabbits ran ;
    A squirrel darted out of sight ;
A heron flew towards fair Lough Dan :
And, far off, in the blue sea-span,
    The white gulls wheeled in tireless flight.

I saw the old arbutus trees ;
    The laurels nigh to the chimney tops ;
About the walks still buzzed the bees ;
And the tangled flowers clung round my knees
    As the tangles in the briary copse.

I looked on it all, and all alone ;
    There was no one there to smile or sigh :
The house was still as a moss-green stone ;
And the echo mocked me, Ochone ! Ochone !
    When I called the beloved of the days gone by.

No face I found, nor voice, nor clue,
    Of the life, the sweet old life, gone by ;
And the sun sank low, and the shadows grew,
Till the place seemed haunted (and I did too)
    By a something which would not in quiet lie.

Then my heart grew hot and began to swell,
    For the ruined dreams of a vanished day,
And I would have cursed ; but anon there fell,
The tinkling tones of the chapel bell ;
    And I turned, and crossed me, and came away.

REQUIESCAT

From the battle's smoke and roar,
Take him back to Erin's shore.

Take him to the green, still land,
Where the gold gorse hems the strand.

Leave his slurs at England's quay;
Leave his stains in God's great sea.

Let her meet him when 'tis dim,
Land he loved as none loved him.

Every carping thought unsaid,
Lay him by the laurelled dead.

Pray, of charity, for his rest;
And throw shamrocks on his breast.—

Out there in the green, still land
Where the gold gorse hems the strand,

Tear-dimmed, with a trembling smile,
His land, which he lost awhile.

Whisper low, where cold he lies,
" Scars fade when the stars arise ; "

Else look down and only pray ;
Erin's idol clasps the clay.

Let that green sod do the rest :
Fold him back to Erin's breast.

Green there let his memory dwell
Baffled, broken, brave Parnell !

The Wooing of Elliana

I.

ELLIANA was her name ;
Out of the Palace of Dreams she came.

From the Palace of Dreams, straight to the throng
Went Elliana singing a song.

Her wild hair floated a golden cloud ;
Her eyes were as stars to the staring crowd.

Wondrous willowy, filmily fair,
Floated her form with her floating hair.

A picture of beauty, a rhythm of grace,
With her lily neck and her rose-leaf face,

She sang to the rude and careless throng
Of the Palace of Dreams by the River of Song.

To look on her made the folk rejoice ;
But they said she'd a poor little tiny voice.

Moreover they called the song she sung
" Outlandish stuff in a foreign tongue."

Now Elliana sang to the throng,
In the language they speak by the River of Song.

Would I could write it, and you could read ;
Translating that tongue is a task indeed.

Where art thou that came from the isle
     Whence hither come I ?
They said thou wouldst meet me and smile
     Ere others drew nigh.

I see not thy face ; and they told me,
     For me thou didst sigh—
Thy care and thy love would enfold me,
     Ere careworn was I.

Where art thou that dost not behold me,
　　Whom once I did see,
A king in the isle where they told me
　　Thy queen I should be—

In the island of sleep where that strong
　　River surges and beams,
To spray into fountains of song
　　By the Palace of Dreams.

When Elliana had sung her song
Silent she quitted the gazing throng.

Wretched was she and sore distressed
At the way men stared at her arms and breast.

The tears stole into her eyes so mild,
The first she had wept since a little child:

In the Palace of Dreams how should she weep—
On the River of Song, in the Isle of Sleep?

There she had slept and dreamed and sung;
For they sing in their sleep there—do the young!

So Elliana cried in the street,
When a lady came to her fair and sweet.

A gentleman next had something to say ;
Then youths and maidens and children gay.

Now it's odd, and beyond all explanations ;
But these people said they were her relations.

So they took Elliana by the hand,
To lead her away to a mansion grand.

When lo and behold, a new surprise
Astonished the people's ears and eyes.

Nigh unto where that maiden sung
They had recently buried a man still young.

'Tis doubtful if he was really dead ;
But " Life had gone out of him," so he said.

"Of its boons and burdens he would be rid ;
They might as well bury him "—so they did.

Some rumour had said that this young man
Had "a mint of gold in a silver pan."

But the wise and rich, in those parts, said,
" In their belief he were better dead."

So they laid him kindly down to rest
With his silver pan, at his own request.

'Tis true that they first examined the pan,
And murmured, " What rubbish ! the poor young
  man ! "

" Well, really ! " they said, and they looked again ;
" What rubbish : it's only the pan of his brain ! "

Now strange as it is—the strangest thing,
Ere Elliana had ceased to sing,

The people standing by that man's grave,
Perceived what is called a terrestrial wave—-

(For there, as with other folks and races
Men buried themselves in the queerest places.)

A wave—a motion they won't forget ;
Some of those people were quite upset,

While others said, and will still repeat,
That the shock carried them off their feet.

He had wished to be buried ; but now 'twas plain
That he meant to be seen alive again.

Down to the depths of his deep, cold bed,
Into his soul and heart and head,

Pulseless, unpeopled of dreams so long,
Went Elliana's dream-worded song.

Only the man as good as dead
Thrilled at her voice— knew what she said.

And up he came from his deep-dug rest,
With many a sob of his heaving chest.

He caught one glimpse of the singer's grace—
Of her lily neck and her rose-leaf face ;

And the vision vanished—filmily fair,
Vanished the cloud of her golden hair.

The people gasped "She has gone" they said ;
" And Heaven forgive us, if you weren't dead !"

" Dead to that voice ?   She *shall* not go !
Dream of my dreams !" he cried ; and lo—

I cannot explain this thing at all ;
On the stage they would let the curtain fall—

The people had vanished : Proud and grand,
Smiling he held Elliana's hand.

But where, it is not for me to tell—
In a village street, or in Pall Mall ;

Hyde Park, or a boulevard Parisian ;
He said it was in the haunts Elysian.

That would seem nonsense.   But what of this :—
" A year were too short to exchange a kiss."

That he said to her—perhaps with his eyes ;
" 'Twere a year well employed," she answered, in
    sighs.

Such was their meeting and conversation,
So far as the writer has information.

He owns it is scant, and a puzzle sore ;
And whether a day or a week or more,

They walked and sat and said—with their eyes—
Such curious things is a theme for the wise.

They haply could tell him by rote and rule ;
At such riddles he owns he's a bit of a fool.

But this he knows that they said "goodbye "
Unkissed, and beneath the open sky.

The sky was cloudy with signs of rain,
The street and the throng had returned again.

" You've been in the Palace," said she ; " You've
      sung " ;
" Ah, child," he answered, " you're very young."

" The world," she murmured, " is not what I
      thought " ;
" You must teach it," he answered, " and not be
      taught."—

"Yes I've been in the Palace," said she; "that's
    plain."
He smiled on her: "When shall we meet again?"

She murmured: "I hope——" then paused and
    smiled;
He waited; and some one exclaimed, "My child!"

"Do you know how the time's gone? Do you
    know
What we've to do, and where we've to go?"

Aside the voice whispered, "And he's a king;
"She's young to begin that sort of thing;

"And she's not begun well with her little flirta-
    tions:"
'Twas the voice of one of her new relations.

"Goodbye, Elliana"—"Goodbye," said she.
"Alas, I'm alone!"—"My child, who's *he?*"

They heard not each other who moaned and
    chided;
How should they, who then were by worlds
    divided?

And immediately after that sad farewell—
Another strange thing—the darkness fell !

The people had vanished, the street, the light :
The man was alone ; and it was night.

The River of Song flowed at his feet ;
Round him the stars throbbed calm and sweet.

He looked on the star-lit glassy tide :
" Would Elliana were at my side ! "

Before him shone, in the moon's white beams,
The many windowed Palace of Dreams :

" Alas," he murmured, " How cold and wan ;
Whither has Elliana gone ? "

Rapt in a reverie sad and deep,
He paced the shore of the Isle of Sleep :

" The voice was hers, the eyes, the hair—
The vision of old, melodious fair !

" Why did she come to me, looked for long,
A rhythm of beauty—embodied song ;

"Only to leave me, trod of the crowd,
A lark's song hushed in a melting cloud ?"

He sighed, " Elliana, my woe is deep,"
And he paced the shore of the Isle of Sleep—

The isle that men knew not, tho' some have said—
What madness !—he paced up and down in his bed.

II.

Annie Ellen now her name,
Out of the Palace of Dreams who came.

Into a mansion spacious, grand,
They led her, who loved her, by the hand,

She had sweet large eyes, complexion fair,
And a knot of beautiful, shining hair.

Her loving and much loved new relations
En route had affected these alterations.

"And now, my child, in this world of care,
The trouble is, first, what you must wear."

So they robed and bedecked her with cost and
    taste,
They padded and puffed her, and *would* have
    tight-laced,

" But, that "—('twas her first wrong word)—she
    said,
" She'd bear not, altho' she'd to live in bed."

She cried and they kissed her : " My pet, you
    know,
Il faut souffrir pour être beau."

But Elliana shook her head :
"'That's not the French I've learned," she said.

" In the Palace of Dreams we learned from France
Came grace and chivalry and romance."

But they loved her, her new relations, much ;
And the maid loved them ; and their love was
    such

That it grew with time through the complications
Of the most remarkable situations,

Until enthroned on a grand settee,
Suitors they brought her to bow the knee.

They bowed and smiled; they flattered and
    fawned;
Chatted and laughed; some even yawned.

Many admired her; some did not;
Some of them did not care a jot—

"'Twas time they were married," those men were
    told—
"And the girl had breeding, and looks, and gold."

And variously they went away,
One to the bottle, and one to the play;

Stolidly some, some heaved a sigh,
One asked for a pin to remember her by.

One fled to a tale of delectable crimes,
And two to the *Matrimonial Times*.

One only had been of that motley squad
Whom Ellen had looked at—except to nod.

She had nodded and smiled and murmured " No,"
Till suitors invited declined to go.

For that one alone her eyes had shone,
A middle-aged, spectacled college don.

To him Elliana even sung ;
For he muttered a word in her native tongue.

On books linguistic he'd feed and sup ;
But where had he picked *that* sentence up ?

Thoughtful ; he'd travelled ; it almost seems
He had peeped thro' a chink of the Palace of
    Dreams,

He loved the maiden ; and when he'd to go,
Elliana gave him her sweetest " No."

And she wanted to give him—a secret this
(For it made a commotion)—to give him a kiss.

And so the days and folk went by ;
And Elliana began to sigh.

Studied she had, and striven too,
The proper things to say, to do;

Blunders had made ; approval found—
Mode-whipped, had toiled through Pleasure's
    round.

And then she sighed.   From scorn forbear,
Brave damsels in " Life's wear and tear."

Pity her maids, who love the strife ;
She wearied in your " Battle of Life."

And one could not for ever find
Trifles to fill her hands and mind.

Tho' human pains came fast and thick,
Folk are not always sad or sick.

Nor came the children's wants and pain
Ofter and surer than the rain—

Times when, indeed, by night and day,
Sleepless, she gloried in the fray,

Emerging with a flower or rattle,
Trophies of all she'd found of *battle*.

She wearied in the noonday heat ;
She sighed in the moonlight cool and sweet—

Sickened, as none can understand,
Not sick of the sweets of a foreign land.

Her fair face drooped on her lily neck—
Each pale-red rose now a blood-rose speck.

Restless upon her couch she lay,
Wishing for night, bearing the day.

Pensive she lay on her bed by night,
Bearing the darkness, wishing for light—

Sighing, wearying for the gleams
Of the radiant soul-thronged Palace of Dreams.—

Wearying, sighing her soul to steep
In the River of Song by the Isle of Sleep.

III.

Carmenartis was his name,
Out of the Palace of Dreams he came.

From the Palace of Dreams, straight to the throng
Went Carmenartis, singing a song.

His eye was piercing, and broad and fair
The forehead fringed with his raven hair.

Sweet was his face when he sang, and when
He smiled 'twas the smile that ruleth men.

And the people gave ear to the song he sung;
For he sang to them in their native tongue.

The critics said, some, that he lacked an ear;
And some that his voice was strong and clear.

The wise ones applauded: they said he had passion,
So a fool clapped his hands, and called him the
fashion.

Then Fashion applauded, and said he was wise;
And the people applauded him to the skies.

Now the song he sang is very well known;
'Tis the fashion still, from the cot to the throne.

For he sang to men about mankind,
Of what he had found and had though to find;

Of the many-coloured, strange-figured breath,
Life, throbbing itself into white, still death;

Of its boons and banes, of its goals and snares,
Of its bladed wheat, and its sheaves and tares,

Of its wealth of love, for the young and hoary,
What he'd seen of fame and had *heard* of glory.

He knew what would make men laugh and weep;
For he'd sailed the world from the Isle of Sleep.

From the River of Song by the Palace of Dreams
He had trafficked on Life's dull wharves and
    streams.

Strange had his mode of traffic been;
Some things he'd felt, some only seen.

Gems he had *found*; and—rather queer—
Loads as of stone had cost him dear.

Then back with his chattels, a curious heap,
Off he had sailed to the Isle of Sleep.

What he did there with them *nobody* knows—
Not makers of dyes and *essence-de-roses*.

He said he "digested them "—very strange thing :
It might have been food—"and it made him sing."

He said that "it *made* him; and that's why the throng
Had heard and applauded his little song."

Moreover he said that it might be long
Ere he anchored again in the River of Song.

" Embargos sad," said he, with a smile,
" Oft closed the ports of his native isle."

Carmenartis had sung his song,
And elbowed him out of the staring throng.

"See," said the folk, "there goes the man
With a mint of gold in a silver pan."

Every street and turn knew he,
Knew where he was, and wished to be.

Round about and through the town
Went Carmenartis up and down,

Asking all folks high and low,
"Where did Elliana go?"

And the answers he received
Oft perplexed him, sometimes grieved.

"Tell me," said he, "tell me where
Went that maid with golden hair?"

"Golden fiddlesticks," they said,
"Brown or flaxen, turning red.

"How can we tell? What's she like?
Could she dance well? Did she bike?

"Weren't there heaps of golden-haired ones—
Slim and fat ones, single, paired ones?

"Gone? Gone everywhere! Hi ho!
Sing us something, don't you know."

"I should think so, my dear boy,"
Said the ladies' last new toy.

"Oft I've seen your priceless pearl—
Rather! she's a rippin' girl!

"See my photos; and then sing,
Some—you know the sort of thing.

"Oh, why, yes, of course, my child,"
Said the matron bland and mild,

"He must mean that girl who really
Took herself so—so ideally.

"Had she sweet, soft baby eyes,
Always lifted in surprise?

"Must you go? Sing something—do:
Something simple—something true."

" Yes, I've danced with her, *she* knows,
Tore her dress—trod on her toes !

" Lord, you have described her rightly ;
She's an angel, shining brightly !

" Off ! whew ! what a beastly throng !
Hoped you'd sing a hunting song ! "

" Why, I *do* remember now ;
Children liked her—goodness how !

" No ! we don't know where she's got to ;
Such nice hair, and such a lot too !

" Nothing in her but—sweet thing !
Ta-ta.   Could *she* make you sing ? "

So perplexed and sad for long,
Carmenartis in the throng,

Joyless, voiceless on the wing,
Sought for joy to make him sing—

Vainly sought his Elliana
By Life's Pharpar and Abana,

Fashion's shallow babbling throng,
Her who knew the River of Song.

IV.

Carmenartis still his name
Out of the babbling throng who came.

His face and his fame of the world forgot,
At last he had learned Elliana's lot.

Long he had sought her, to find at last,
The fret of life and its fever past,

Cold in a cold, grand mausoleum,
To the wail of the world and the world's *Te Deum*—

Deaf to its Pharpar and Abana,
Motionless, mute, his Elliana!

There they had laid her who lay as dead,
With a golden dome o'er her golden head.

There they had laid her, but did not leave:
" We love her," they said, " and she does not
    grieve.

" She knoweth not sorrow nor pain," they said,
" And the trance will pass, for she is not dead.

" We've but to be patient a little while,
To see her awaken with a smile—

" Awake as she wakes from her trance always,
To the children's laughter in summer days."

And where was that wonderful mausoleum
Where she slept to the world's wail and *Te Deum* ?

Ah, none may tell, but the souls that creep
Round and within it, then fall asleep.

But people of Elliana said,
" She'd not even taken to her bed ;

" She had only gone moping about the house—
What language !—and then grown as still as a
    mouse."

To that mansion grand, Elliana's tomb,
Stole Carmenartis through the gloom.

'Twas night, and a gentle summer breeze
Wandered and sighed among the trees.

Soft, where the shades were deepest thrown,
Stole Carmenartis to sing alone.

" Listen," remarked the passers-by,
" The wind is moaning, a storm is nigh."

Would they had heard the things he said,
Translated they scarcely seem fit to be read :—

How far hast thou strayed from the River
  Whereof is thy fairness the foam !
How far from the isle
Whose gems are thy smile,
  Whose bloom is thy bloom, dost thou roam ?
How far from the music and dance,
Whence thy step and thy voice and thy glance
  Drew their magic and sway,
  In thy childhood at play
On the shore of the isle of thy home ?
    Elliana, only there
    Shalt thou sleep away thy care !

" See," they said, " her eyelid quivers ;
Life returns : she moans and shivers.

" 'Tis the murmuring, sighing breeze ;
'Tis the rustling of the trees.

" Ever did she love to hear them ;
Hush the music : bear her near them."

The River is singing its song,
The Palace of Dreams is aglow :
At its windows, whose bars
Are the beams of the stars—
Its curtains of cloud and of snow,
Is pulsing the throng
Of the souls of song,
Who see and who hear and who know,
Then in gladness and pain
Sow the seed and the grain
Of all that's immortal below !
Behold them preparing it now :
Where, where Elliana art thou ?

And they cried in their joy, " She shall rise :
See, she opens her beautiful eyes !

" Behold now her sobs—her delight."
She smiled : " He has come in the night."

Then they kissed her with clapping of hands :
" She dreams ; but she rises—she stands."

She kissed them : " Ah, now let me weep :
He sings, and he'll sing me to sleep."

" To sleep ?   What a fancy, my child ;
You're waking ! you've wept, and you've smiled ;

" And soon you'll be dancing," they cried.
" My heart has begun," she replied.

" I hear him, shall see him—shall find."
" Sweet angel, she's not lost her mind ? "

" Ah, no ! " and she laughed.   " That were droll,
When I've found—he has brought me my soul."

Behold, by the reeds of the River—
    The reeds that the singers blow,
From the golden marge
The golden barge

Out to the ocean go—
From the isle of inviolate sleep,
O'er the troubled unresting deep,
　With its soul-wrought store,
　To each wreck-strewn shore,
　For the souls of the sleepless that smile no
　　more,
And the sad ones that cannot weep !
　Elliana, from that strand
　Thou shouldst smile and wave thy hand !

" And behold my hand I wave—
　Both my hands, where was my grave !

" And my smiles, with tears, are turned
　To the souls for whom I've yearned.

" Let my outstretched hands be taken—
　Let me long forgot, forsaken,

" Clasped and carried be once more
　To that soul-thronged, graveless shore—

" Song-and-flower-filled, sparkling, vernal,
　Of sweet tears and smiles eternal ! "

Then said they, amazed, aghast,
" 'Tis those fancies of the Past—

" Dreams and hopes—the wild creations
Of her early expectations.

" She would leave us : she would go
Wandering where she does not know."

" List," she cried, " that wondrous chant ! "
" Darling," said they, " that is cant ! "

" Joyous, plaintive, sinking, rising ! "
" Really, Ellen, it's surprising ! "

" Bursts of gladness, sobs and wails ! "
" Foolish fancies, fairy tales ! "

For, said they—one here should mention—
All that song was her invention :

Who such voices never stirred
Said no voice had now been heard—

No man sang hid in the gloom ;
There was neither song nor tomb.

All were fancies—foolish, wild,
Of their poor, sweet, foolish child,

Manufactured day by day
From one idolised *bouquet*,

Sent her by that man who, maybe,
Was her idol—when a baby.

Disembarked, departed, scattered,
See that freight of souls no more ;
Hear no more that peon ringing
Of the starry-souled ones singing
  On the song-washed shining shore !
Look no more where they embark ;
Look throughout the world and hark,
  At the tears and laughs they're making ;
  Hear the melodies they're waking ;
  See them laugh where light is breaking ;
Hear them sobbing in the dark !
  Elliana, they are those
  Who demand thy joys and woes.

" Hark," she said, " their voices call me,
And their melodies enthrall me.

" Longer here I may not linger ! '
" Child," they said, " you're not a singer.

" To that awful, lonely height
Of Ambition's dazzling flight.

" Souls are *born !* " said she.   " My mission
Is of love : 'tis not ambition—

" Love for them here born to climb
Lonely to those heights sublime—

" Love for those who ne'er shall reach them ! "
" Child ! how can *you* help or teach them ? "

" All her mind has turned anew
To that ill-clad, motley crew,

" Dreamers, dotards, fools, fanatics,
Scribbling, singing in their attics,

" And the man who made her love them,
Now enthroned one inch above them.

" Life has duties : life is real."
" Yea," said she, and Life's ideal

" Is at last to find in duty
   The reality of Beauty.

" Hear you not the voices round me
   Of the sweet ghosts that have found me—

" Me to sing and waft once more
   To those haunts and days of yore—

" Golden days ! haunts hymeneal,
   Where souls find the soul's ideal !"

" Really, child, and when were those days ?
   Where do souls behave in those ways ?"

" Haunts of Hymen !   Golden days !
   Talk of ' marriage,' ' settled ways ' !"

" Those, my dear, are serious themes ;
   Not for song and Love's young dreams.

" But the poetry you roll in ;
   And why *must* you drag the *soul* in ?"

And those welcome thronging hosts
Of sweet voices and fair ghosts

By that maiden entertained
"Were" they said—the folks they pained—

(For indeed their disinterment
In that house produced a ferment)—

" But the outcome—nothing better
Of one wretched ill-rhymed letter—

" Signed ('twas madness, rubbish—wrong !)
Carmenartis seeking song."

Follow them, the lonely-hearted
Few, few to be laurel-browed !
For the rapture, now departed,
Feel the stings that long have smarted
From the slights and insults, darted
    At them by the basely proud !
Feel their scorn and know their anger,
Where, with incensed prayer and clangour
    Gemmed lust to gilt dust is bowed !
Know that anger ;
And their langour—
Oh—that languor, dumb and sodden,
Where they languish stifled, trodden

Of the sleep-brained, sheep-led crowd !
Then in want, Despair-bespoken,
See some, shamed with shame's last token,
Follow—kneel—be taught :—They're broken,
  Broken-souled, the vows they vowed !
    Elliana, in Life's city
    These souls need thy love and pity !

Weeping cried she, " Theirs they are—
Theirs—my people, near, afar,

" Sowing, reaping, glad, deploring,
  Tranquil, struggling, failing, soaring,

" Who, of all to-day kept waiting,
  All to-morrows are creating,

" From whose fragile wares, soul-wrought
  Tiny wind-blown webs of thought,

" Spun in Life's dim, lonely nooks,
  Come the woven piles of books—

" Come the sermons, declamations—
  Come the fiery perorations,—

" All of Soul that sways the throng,
　From the crowd-scorned souls of song ! "

" Nay " they cried, then clustering round her,
" *We* your people ! "—who had found her—

" You our child "—who did not know her,
　Wailed, " Why would she wed below her ? "

　Scorned him waked of Elliana
　As Endymion of Diana,

　And now called the voice that charmed her,
　Thrilled, enthralled her, fired her, calmed her,

　But " the last-inflicted torrent
　Of his *billet-doux* abhorrent,

" Asking now—what madness led him—
Goodness ! gracious ! would she wed him ? "

　Star of my haven in Sleep's sweet isle !
　　Source of the song that arose in me !
　It is not the mouth that makes the smile ;
　　Not makers of song men such as we.

Oh, there never had been a song-washed isle,

Had there never been souls, with a voice and
 smile

 To sing through the singers, like to thee !

What were the bells but for them that ring
 them ;

What were the lights but for them that fling
 them,

 Over the land and out on the sea ?

Singer that sang me out of my tomb,

 Soul of all things that are song to me,

Voice that were scorned in the world's mad
 boom,

 The voice I would trumpet across the sea !

Of such are the soul, the voice, the smile

That throb and shine in that radiant isle ;

  And down to the throng—

  It need not be rhymes—

  By the River of Song,

  From all the climes,

  Their message are flinging

  Of smiling and singing

Down the dark vista of woes and crimes—

  Of smiles that shall fade not,

Of song that shall jade not,
Light, music yet made not :—
    Day's dawn and its chimes !
    Elliana, come away ;
    Wouldst thou ever voiceless be ?
    Must I longer songless stray ?
    Elliana, come to me !

And she cried, " My belovèd one's voice !
My soul's long desire and her choice !

" His step !—who henceafter beside me,
Unbaffled, unwearied, shall guide me.

" His face !—at whose smile, as the deep
For the moon's, will I languish and leap.

" His arms !—wherewith I to his breast
Shall be drawn, as the day to the west—

" Wherein, let days gallop or creep,
Will I shine or repine me, and sleep.

" To thine arms, my belovèd, I hasten :
Let them fold, if Life gladden or chasten ;

" Let them bind whate'er loose or hold fast ;
Let them find me, beloved, at the last ! "

So she straight uncontrollably fled ;
And they watched her, the wise ones, and said,

" What now ? and why—where has she flown ? "
Who voice nor step heard but their own.

And anon they said, " Listen, oh dear !
Those are wheels on the gravel : He's here ! "

V.

Carmenelli was their name ;
Out of the babbling throng they came.

To the Palace of Dreams, straight from the
    throng
Went Carmenelli, singing a song.

Her wild hair floated a cloud of gold
To the eyes they illumined with dreams of old.

Steadfast and sweet as the stars above
Were his eyes to the face that they filled with
    love.

Firm as a cedar, filmily fair ;
Strong as a pillar ; and light as air !

The power of beauty, of strength the charm,
The lily neck in the oaken arm.

Her rose-leaf cheek to his bronze cheek
    pressed :—
Love's garnered bloom on its mailèd breast.

So Carmenelli, beautiful, strong,
Floated and swung themselves out of the throng,

For beauty and strength—where they hold them
    cheap—
To traffic and trade in the Isle of Sleep,

And ship them to ports upon Life's dull streams
Down the River of Song, from the Palace of
    Dreams.

" And where are those haunts ? " is it asked
    again :
Who asketh in scorn will ask in vain.

And the people said who had seen them off,
Some with a sigh and some with a scoff,

Some with a giggle, some petful and harried,
" Thanks be to goodness : They're done with and
    married ! "

Pot=Pourri

---·×·---

HER CHARMS

IT is not that her face is fair
 Above all mortal faces ;
It is not that still lingers there
 A charm from childhood's graces.

It is not that her smiles, like light,
 Illume the hearts that love her—
Her eyes so blue, and not too bright,
 Are like the stars above her.

It is not this, nor that, nor aught
 Of isolated sweetness ;
'Tis something Love throughout has wrought
 To beautiful completeness.

A something we can not define—
    An influence about her,
That renders things in her divine,
    Which were not so without her.

Even as scenes not rare grow rare
    When sunset hues have crowned them,
Her graces shine supremely fair
    In that pure light around them.

MISSING

Sometimes I wish, without delay
  To cross that strip of sea—
Be in those old, sweet haunts the self-same day;
  And that, perchance, might be :

I might to-night find each fair peak
  In the soft moonlight there—
The old white house and you ; yet what I seek
  Might still be otherwhere

How oft, how sadly is it so?—
  We re-create with care
Some vanished place and day, to find and know
  Our old selves are not there.

LA FÉE BOITEUSE

BECAUSE they made our parting sore,
  Who knew we had to part,
We'll meet and talk hence evermore,
  And wander, heart by heart.

And since to thee I must not write—
  The world says 'twould not do—
Straight to their world I this indite,
  And send my love to you,

Their world in which thou mayst not dance,
  Tho' scarce of earth—a fay
Caught here, and doubly chained, perchance,
  Lest thou shouldst float away—

Their world ! my dear, when troubled still,
 Asleep 'twill groan and snore,
We'll have *our* world, and dance until
 Theirs sleeps to dance no more.

We'll never say, nor feel, goodbye :
 That is for joy that's been—
For old loves that might tire or die,
 Should new loves come between.

Goodbye ? We know our trysting star,
 Let millions stud the blue ;
In love or not, at home, afar,
 You can find me—I, you.

And we've our pledge—our secret ? nay,
 We'll let the wise world know :
My love was open as the day
 And yours pure as the snow.

And as the worn day, stained, alack,
 Kisses the snow-peak white,
I kissed you, and you kissed me back :
 " Sweet dreams, sweetheart—good-night."

POSTSCRIPT

WRITTEN MANY YEARS LATER

EDITH, because the world's eyes, nor its tongue,
　　Nor time, nor change
My heart, more aged and thine, for ever young,
　　Can yet estrange—

Because we've still sweet talks and loved walks
　　lonely,
　　Warned of the wise—
(What folly have *theirs* wrought since met once
　　only
　　Our lips and eyes?)

Because I think (tho' but in dreams and letters
　　Now reprobates)
Some day to find my fairy, and her fetters
　　Love's open gates,

I give the wise my mind for wisdom's sake;
　　But if there be
Lips welcome, from my heart the kisses take
　　Which I send thee.

IN ANSWER TO VERSES CONTAINING AN OFFER OF MARRIAGE—D'ESPRIT

Fair type of the States
  Y-clept the United,
When minds live as mates
  Say how are they plighted?

Tho' you scarce seem of clay—
(One might call you a fay,)
I should guess you nine stone;
And for me, tho' I'm spare,
I'm not light as air,
  And not short of a bone!

Would you then be a ghost?
I an essence at most?

'Twere a difficult *rôle*.
And I'd ask for my part,
Should I still own my heart,
    When you'd leased me your soul ?

But suppose we were wed ;
Say our bodies were dead—
    I mean deaf, dumb, and blind,
Then for what sort of nook
For our home should we look ?
    What sort should we find ?
Think of fixtures and fittings,
(Not to speak of the flittings)
    When mind marries mind !

Thus to live would bring blisses :
When I think of the kisses,
    Oh, I want to commence :
But fears come unending : --
"Things always want mending ! "
" Then the saving and spending—
    Of psychical pence ! "
Your soul might go moping,
Mine doubting and hoping,
Till one went eloping
    With—somebody's sense !

Ah me, I confess
I should like to say "yes";
But I know that my mind
Is not of the kind
   That would bear such a strain !
It annoys me each day ;
If the truth I must say,
   It's both stupid and vain !
And my body's not dead,
It could soon lose its head—
   It has lost it before ;
But it always comes back,
And alack, dear, alack,
   Just as stupid and more !

My dear, it were sweet
Still to sit at your feet,
Still to bask in your rays,
And to walk in your ways,
   To run with you courses
Of beautiful days ;
But I think you must see
That folks loving as we
   Should drive single horses

And count themselves free ;
For you own, dear, you fly
Straight to men such as I ;
And for me, if I see
And can grasp what would be,
    I've had several divorces
From marriage—*d'esprit.*

WHAT is beauty but the flashing
   From a flower in sunlight gay?
What is wit, say, but the splashing
   From a fountain's falling spray?

What is there in being clever?
   What in being very wise?
Eminence is bleak for ever:
   Knowledge brings us many sighs.

What these gifts, and those who own them,
   Unto one whose worth I know,
One whose life might well have shown them,
   Having all from which they grow?

Hers the sunlight, not the glitter;
  Hers the fountain, not the spray :—
Skill to make sweet things from bitter;
  Knowledge to make sad ones gay.

Many wise there are, and witty;
  Many clever as we would;
Many more superbly pretty;
  But how many purely good?

Her in childhood's bright beginning,
  Nature loved, and said 'twere meet
Once to make one wholly winning—
  Make one solely, simply sweet.

ONCE AGAIN

Unto my Transatlantic children far,
Paternal greetings and the kiss—I'm raving !
My dears, I've just been wondering how you are ;
And also wondering, as your English pa,
   How you're behaving.

The spring has come again : the butterfly
Will soon be on the wing, and so shall I—
Don't press beyond due limits that comparison ;
Tho' bookworms are but embryo moths, you know,
And fairly fledged you don't know where they'll go :
   See Fr-d-k H-r-i-son.
But I would go where I've been oft of yore
(Straight as the swallow flies from shore to shore)

To pines and mountains,

To snow - peaks, pathless hills, and vine - clad
    valleys—

White winding roads, bright lakes, and mist-blue
    alleys,

    And foaming fountains.

Then tell me, dears, where you'll be passing by,

That I may catch you *à la* butterfly,

I bookless and but busy with things gay,

You like the flowers—I mean sweet things—at
    play.

    The world grows cold ;

Let mem'ry snatch, then, one more sunny day
    For when we're old.

How do you like the notion, *mes petites ?*

Say, do you cross the Rhone to gain the Fleet,
    From Afric's shore ?

And if we are to meet on earth once more,
    Where shall it be—

Montreux ? Genève ? Some old sweet *rendez-*
    vous ?

Or might we have a flutter 'neath the blue
    In *beau Paris ?*

Adieu !   Just tell me when you take your flight—
Now you're the butterflies and I—good-night :
'Tis now too late to tell you what *I* am,
Except " yours truly "—in a world of sham.
My lamp is burning low : Once more good-night,
Just now, the stars and your goodbyes shine bright,
Things beautiful, which oft, at close of day,
Speak both of flitting smiles and bright worlds far
    away.

OTHERWISE

A STRANGER mute at *table d'hôte*,
  Of late made sad and wise;
But I marked the whiteness of your throat,
  And the blueness of your eyes.

A pleasant voice; a gracious wit;
  Maid of a kindred land :—
My numbed heart stirred a little bit
  At the first touch of your hand.

A frank smile when we met; a chat;
  A ramble by the Rhone :—
Then gossips in the throng we sat;
  Then often mute alone.

Talk, silence, smiles, with no eclipse
　　Of interest ; then goodbye :—
Our hearts had touched, but, not our lips :
　　Love's dream dreamed you nor I.

Now years have flown ; but your white throat
　　From revery's mists will rise ;
And oft, at Memory's *table d'hôte*,
　　I look at your blue eyes.

Again we talk, grow mute, and smile,
　　On fair Lake Leman's shore ;
Why did we draw so close awhile,
　　To part for evermore ?

Again to me you say " goodbye ";
　　And on life lifeless slips :—
Why did they meet—our hearts ; or why
　　Our hearts, and not our lips ?

Miscellaneous

—◆—

REMEMBERED FACES

SOME faces are supinely fair,
  Some sparkling in their splendour,
Some are demure and debonair,
  And some divinely tender.

Some win us with one fatal glance,
  From eyes too brightly beaming ;
Some smile that smile that brings a trance
  Till life is lost in dreaming.

Some flit before us, sweet and gay,
  To fill our hearts with laughter,
Then fade as fancies fade away,
  And leave no aching after.

So faces come and faces go ;
   Some make existence sweeter ;
And some, they make life sad, we know,
   And being sad, completer.

Until her face comes up at last
   (Heaven knows each heart : don't doubt it)—
The Future fades, the Past is past !
   We love each line about it.

We ask not if men call her sweet,
   Or fair, or wise, or clever ;
We ask and sometimes we repeat,
   " Will you be mine for ever ? "

ALTERED

Life's sad awakenings with a sense of pain,
　　To which one rises,
Are mostly dull, cold whispers of the brain,
　　And not surprises.

The eyes that shone with love still brightly shine,
　　The lips still smile ;
Nor we, nor those around us can divine
　　A shadow of guile.

We say "goodbye," and neither heart can show
　　Where Love has faltered ;
Only, when left alone, one sighs to know
　　That things are altered.

It rains in the morning ; it rains at night ;
    And all the day ;
On the roofs and the road, on the fields which
    white
    To harvest sway.
It rains while the farmers murmur and mutter,
It rains thro' the prayers the parsons utter,
    It rains alway.
It rains on the sad and increases their sorrow ;
    And on the gay ;
On those who are sure 'twill be sunny to-morrow ;
On those who this comfort don't easily borrow,
    But hope it may !
It rains in the city, the slimy streets,
    Packed, dense and grey ;
It rains in the country, the still retreats,
    Where tourists stray.

It rains whatsoever we wish to see ;
It rains thro' the land wherever we be—
      At work or play ;
And out on the rain-made sopping sea,
      It rains for aye !
It rains and it rains and it rains till we,
      For once in a way,
Might think that in Lucifer's home they'd be—
      Well—making hay !

THE SECRET OF BEAUTY

I COULD not tell—I do not know
    What classic lines, what curves of grace
Must meet, and blend and intergrow
    To make for me a beauteous face.

I do not know—I could not tell,
    With all the lines and curves complete,
What look within that face must dwell
    To make *me* find its beauty *sweet*.

Unknown the laws that make it sweet,
    And flower-like mould it as it grows;
Enough that when that face I meet,
    I know it as I know the rose !

INCOMPATIBILITY

And what is "song" that well-like springs
   Sometimes in such as he ?—
That light he called "God's smile" that clings
   Sometimes to such as she ?

A phase of life—a fleeting phase
   To discipline the heart :—
All lives learn lessons in such ways,
   To teach souls how to part.

Let them be still : That song, that light
   Will not enthrall them long—
Will not enrapture or affright,
   Be they but calm and strong.

Let them be still and wait: Again
    Life will give all they ask ;
If little joy, then less the pain ;
    Small gain, more brief the task !

Let them but wait, and hear the wise :—
    " See how we get along :
God's smile ?   Yea, surely in the skies ;
    There life will be a song."

" But here such Love a troubled dream ;
    Dream it, and let it go."
Listen : " Such joy a fitful gleam " ;
    They speak that they do know.

Listen : " Rare bliss a doubtful boon,"
    Perhaps, and cannot stay ;
But *will* God give hearts back so soon
    That Heaven they've flung away?

THE MAIDEN OF THE MIST

He had hunted the forest hoar and vast ;
  He had dragged the dim, deep lake ;
Afar he had wandered, his eyes wide cast,
For the path he had lost, till he sighed at last
  To die on the yellow brake.

So he sat and stared at the shimmering tide ;
  When, far from its golden rim,
A coracle came whose oars were plied
By a beautiful maiden, who reached his side
  As his spell-bound eyes grew dim.

" Behold me," she cried, " who for me hast sighed,"
  And a voice moaned in his brain,
" Behold, but resist : 'Tis the garb of the Mist,
The face of the woods of the sunset kissed,
  And the sweet voice of the rain."

But he leaped in the boat, and away they sailed;
  And he smiled at a chain on his wrist;
And out on the tide, the maid's cheek paled :—
She sighed, and they sank; and the man's heart
    wailed,
  "'Tis the Maiden of the Mist."

And never a wrack of that boat came back;
  But, bared of the drifted sand,
In the years long after and now no more,
A traveller started, on that wan shore,
  At an outstretched skeleton hand.

And round the wrist was a golden chain,
  And pressed to the palm a stone,
And in the stone, preserved from stain,
Was a petal of bloom, where these words remain,
  In the language he had known :—

"Through the Forest of Years, o'er the Lake of
    Tears,
  She cometh to break thy chain,
Who is strong and true as thy bow of yew,
And as pure and sweet as the sun and dew,
  And as gracious as the rain."